ROBINSON CRUSOE FOR CHILDREN

DANIEL DEFOE

ROBINSON CRUSOE

WRITTEN ANEW FOR CHILDREN

WITH APOLOGIES TO

DANIEL DEFOE

BY

JAMES BALDWIN

YESTERDAY'S CLASSICS

CHAPEL HILL, NORTH CAROLINA

ISBN-10: 1-59915-180-4

ISBN-13: 978-1-59915-180-9

Yesterday's Classics
PO Box 3418
Chapel Hill, NC 27515

TO

THE TWO LITTLE LADIES

WHO HELP TO MAKE OUR SUMMERS AT

BREIDABLIK

A SUCCESSION OF

BROAD BLINKS OF DELIGHT

THIS NEW OLD STORY IS AFFECTIONATELY

INSCRIBED

BY THEIR LOVER, PLAYMATE

AND GRANDPAPA

FOREWORD

In the year 1719 an Englishman whose name was Daniel Defoe wrote a very long story, which he called "The Life and Surprising Adventures of Robinson Crusoe." His story was not designed for children, and therefore it contained a great deal of hard reading. There was much in it, however, that was interesting to young people, and from that day to this, the marvelous tale of Robinson Crusoe has been a favorite with boys as well as men. I have rewritten the story in words easy for every child, and have shortened it by leaving out all the dull parts.

HOW MY STORY RUNS

I WISH TO BE A SAILOR

My name is Robinson Crusoe. I was born in the old city of York, where there is a broad river, with ships coming and going.

When I was a little boy, I spent much of my time looking at the river.

How pleasant was the quiet stream, flowing, always flowing, toward the far-away sea!

I liked to watch the ships as they came in with their white sails spread to the wind.

I liked to think of the strange lands which they must have visited, and of the many wonderful things they must have passed.

I wished to be a sailor. I thought how grand it must be to sail and sail on the wide blue sea, with the sky above and the waves beneath. Nothing could be pleasanter.

My father wanted me to learn a trade. But I could not bear the thought of it. I could not bear the thought of working every day in a dusty shop.

I did not wish to stay in York all my life. I wanted to see the world. I would be a sailor and nothing else.

My mother was very sad when I told her.

A sailor's life, she said, was a hard life. There were many storms at sea, and ships were often wrecked.

She told me, too, that there were great fishes in the sea, and that they would eat me up if I fell into the water.

Then she gave me a cake, and kissed me. "How much safer it is to be at home!" she said.

But I would not listen to her. My mind was made up, and a sailor I would be.

When I was eighteen years old, I left my pleasant home and went to sea.

I MAKE MY FIRST VOYAGE

I SOON found that my mother's words were true. A sailor's life is indeed a hard life.

There was no time for play on board of our ship. Even in the fairest weather there was much work to be done.

On the very first night the wind began to blow. The waves rolled high. The ship was tossed this way and that. Never had I seen such a storm.

All night long the wind blew. I was so badly frightened that I did not know what to do. I thought the ship would surely go to the bottom.

Then I remembered my pleasant home and the words of my kind mother.

"If I live to reach dry land," I said to myself, "I will give up this thought of being a sailor. I will go home and stay with my father and mother. I will never set my foot in another ship."

Day came. The storm was worse than before. I felt sure that we were lost. But toward evening the sky began to clear. The wind died away. The waves went down. The storm was over.

The next morning the sun rose bright and warm upon a smooth sea. It was a beautiful sight.

As I stood looking out over the wide water, the first mate came up. He was a kind man, and always friendly to me.

"Well, Bob," he said, "how do you like it? Were you frightened by that little gale?"

"I hope you don't call it a little gale," I said. "Indeed it was a terrible storm."

The mate laughed.

"Do you call that a storm?" he asked. "Why, it was nothing at all. You are only a fresh-water sailor, Bob. Wait till we have a real storm."

And so I soon forgot my fears.

Little by little, I gave up all thoughts of going home again. "A sailor's life for me," I said.

My first voyage was not a long one.

I visited no new lands, for the ship went only to London. But the things which I saw in that great city seemed very wonderful to me.

Nothing would satisfy me but to make a long voyage. I wished to see the whole world.

I SEE MUCH OF THE WORLD

IT was easy to find a ship to my liking; for all kinds of trading vessels go out from London to every country that is known.

One day I met an old sea captain who had been often to the coast of Africa. He was pleased with my talk.

"If you want to see the world," he said, "you must sail with me." And then he told me that he was going again to Africa, to trade with the black people there. He would carry out a load of cheap trinkets to exchange for gold dust and feathers and other rare and curious things.

I was very glad to go with him. I would see strange lands and savage people. I would have many a stirring adventure.

Before ten days had passed, we were out on the great ocean. Our ship was headed toward the south.

The captain was very kind to me. He taught me much that every sailor ought to know. He showed me how to steer and manage the vessel. He told me about the tides and the compass and how to reckon the ship's course.

The voyage was a pleasant one, and I saw more wonderful things than I can name.

When, at last, we sailed back to London, we had gold enough to make a poor man rich.

I had nearly six pounds of the yellow dust for my own share.

I had learned to be a trader as well as a sailor.

It would take too long to tell you of all my voyages. Some of them were happy and successful; but the most were unpleasant and full of disappointment.

Sometimes I went to Africa, sometimes to the new land of South America. But wherever I sailed I found the life of a sailor by no means easy.

I did not care so much now to see strange sights and visit unknown shores.

I cared more for the money or goods that I would get by trading.

At last a sudden end was put to all my sailing. And it is of this that I will now tell you.

I UNDERTAKE A NEW VENTURE

I HAD grown very tired of being a sailor. I was so tired of it that I made up my mind to try something else.

It happened that I was then in Brazil. I bought some land there and began to open a plantation. The ground was rich, and it would be easy to raise tobacco and sugar cane.

But I needed many things. I must have plows and hoes and a sugar mill. Above all I must have men to do the work on the plantation.

But neither men nor tools could I get in Brazil.

I sent to London for the tools. I tried to buy some slaves of the planters near me, but they had not enough for themselves.

"We will tell you what to do," they said. "We will fit out a trading vessel for Africa. We will put aboard of it everything that you need. As for your part, you shall be the manager of the business; and you shall do the trading for us. You need not put in a penny of your own."

"But how is that going to help me?" I asked.

"Listen, and we will tell you," they said. "With the goods which we send, you will buy as many black slaves as the ship will hold. You will bring them here, and we will divide them equally. You shall share with us, just as though you had paid the money."

The plan pleased me very much. I figured that each one of us would have thirty or forty slaves.

It was very foolish of me to go to sea again; but the offer was so good that I could not say No.

The ship was soon fitted out for the voyage. Her load was not very heavy. But there were plenty of goods such as were most fit for trade.

There were boxes of red and blue beads, of bits of glass, and of other trinkets. There were also knives and hatchets and little looking-glasses. We reckoned that each one of these would buy a slave.

The ship was to carry fourteen men besides the captain and myself. She was as fine a little vessel as ever sailed from the coast of Brazil.

8

I AM SHIPWRECKED

At length all things were ready for the voyage, and I went on board the ship.

It was just eight years to the day since I had left my father and mother and my pleasant home in good old York.

I felt that I was doing a foolish thing; but I did not dare to say so.

The wind was fair. The sails were spread. Soon we were out to sea.

For several days the weather was fine. The ship sped swiftly on her way, and every one was happy and hopeful.

Then a great storm came up from the southeast. I had seen many a fierce storm, but never one so terrible as this.

We could do nothing but let the ship drive before the wind. Day after day we were tossed by the waves; and day after day we expected the ship to go down.

The storm grew fiercer and fiercer. The men gave themselves up as lost.

But on the twelfth day the wind went down. The waves were not so strong. We began to hope for our lives.

Early the next morning a sailor cried out, "Land! land!"

I ran out of the cabin to look. But at that very moment the ship struck upon a great bank of sand over which the fierce sea was rolling.

She stopped short. She could not move. The great waves dashed over her deck. All of us would have been washed overboard if we had not hurried back to the cabin.

"What shall we do?" cried the men.

"We can do nothing," said the captain. "Our voyage is at an end, and there is no longer any hope for our lives. We can only wait for the ship to break in pieces."

"Yes, there is one chance for our lives," cried the mate. "Follow me!"

In the lull of the storm we rushed again to the deck. One of our boats was still there.

We slung her over the ship's side. We jumped aboard of her. We cut her loose, and floated away upon the wild sea.

No boat could live in such a sea as that. But we saw land ahead of us; and perhaps some of us might be cast alive upon the beach.

This was our only hope.

The raging waves carried us nearer and nearer to the shore.

We could see the breakers dashing upon the great rocks. The land looked more frightful than the sea.

Then all at once, a huge wave overset the boat. We had no time to speak or think. We were thrown out into the raging sea. We were swallowed up by the waves.

I AM CAST UPON A STRANGE SHORE

THE next thing I knew I was lying on the beach and the breakers were rolling over me.

Some wave, kinder than others, must have carried me there.

I got upon my feet and ran as fast as I could.

I saw another wave coming after me. It was high as a hill.

I held my breath and waited. In a moment the wave was upon me. I could feel myself carried farther and farther toward the dry land.

The water covered me. But I held my breath and tried to swim.

The wave became smaller and weaker as it rolled farther and farther up the long beach.

At last I could keep my head and shoulders above water. I could breathe again.

I felt the ground under my feet. I struck out with all my might for the dry land.

But now the water was rushing back from the shore. I feared lest I should be carried out to sea again.

I swam, I ran. I held on to the rocks. Then another great wave came and lifted me high upon the shore.

In another moment I was safe on dry land.

All worn out with the hard struggle, I lay down upon the green grass. I looked up at the sky and thanked God that I was alive and safe.

After I had rested a little while I arose and looked around me.

Far out from the shore I could see the ship. It was still lying where it had stuck in the sand. The waves were dashing over it.

"How was it possible for me to swim so far?" I asked myself.

Then I began to think of the men that were with me. Had any of them been saved?

I walked along the shore for a mile or more. I looked in every spot for some signs of my friends.

In one place I found a hat; in another, a cap; And in still another, two shoes that were not mates.

But of the men themselves I saw nothing. All were drowned in the deep sea.

13

I FIND A STRANGE LODGING PLACE

It was now late in the afternoon. The sun was shining in the bright sky. The storm was at an end.

I began to look around me, to see what kind of place I was in. "Where shall I go?" I asked myself. "What shall I do?"

My clothes were still wet. I could dry them only by sitting in the sun.

I had nothing to eat or drink.

I had nothing about me but a knife, a pipe, and a little tobacco.

How could I live on this strange shore without shelter and without food?

The thought of this made me almost wild. I ran this way and that, like a madman.

14

Then I sat down and cried like a child.

I never felt so lonely as at that moment. I never felt so helpless and lost.

Soon I saw that night was coming on.

I thought: "What if there are wild beasts in the woods? They will come out in the darkness and find me here. And then how can I save myself from them?"

A little way from the shore I saw a tree. It stood all alone, with no other trees near it.

It was thick and bushy, with long thorns on its branches.

I walked out to look at it.

To my great joy I found a spring of fresh water bubbling out from among its roots.

I knelt down and took a long drink, for I was very thirsty. Then I climbed up into the tree.

The branches grew very close together. I found a place where I could rest, half sitting and half lying, with no danger of falling.

With my pocket knife I cut a strong stick about two feet long. This would be my weapon if any beast should find me in the night.

It was now quite dark. The only sound that I could hear was that of the waves breaking against the shore.

It seemed so good to be on dry land that I forgot every danger. I was so tired that I soon fell asleep. Never have I slept more soundly.

I VISIT THE WRECK

WHEN I awoke it was broad daylight. The sun was up. The sky was clear. The air seemed soft and mild. A fine day was beginning.

It did not take me long to come down from my lodging place.

I looked out toward the sea.

To my great wonder, I saw that the ship was now much closer to the shore. The high tide had lifted her off the sand. It had carried her toward the land and left her on a huge rock less than a mile away.

I could see that the good ship stood upright and was firmly wedged into the rock.

The waves had not broken her up, but her masts had been snapped off, and all her rigging was gone.

The sea was quite smooth, and the tide was still going out. Soon the beach was bare, and I could walk a long way out.

I was now within a quarter of a mile of the ship.

As I looked at her, a sad thought came to my mind. For if we had all kept on board when she stuck in the sand, we would now have been safe.

But there was no use in thinking of what might have been.

I waded out as far as I could, and then swam for the ship.

As I came near her, I saw that she was lying high out of the water. The part of the rock that was uncovered rose steep and straight into the air. There was no place for me to set my feet.

I swam round the ship twice. How could I ever climb up her smooth sides?

I was about to give up, when I saw a small piece of rope hanging down from the deck. It reached almost to the water. How strange that I did not see it at first!

I seized hold of the rope, and climbed hand over hand to the deck.

I went into the ship's cabin. I looked all through the unlucky vessel.

I MAKE ME A RAFT

THERE was a great deal of water in the ship's hold. But the cabin and the storerooms were dry.

The boxes of food had not been touched by the water.

I was very hungry, but I had no time to lose. So I filled my pockets with dry biscuits and ate them as I went about.

There were many things on the ship. They might be very useful to me if I had them on shore. But there was no boat, and how could I carry them there?

"I will make a raft," I said to myself.

There were several long pieces of timber on the deck. I tied a rope to each of these so that it would not float away. Then I dropped them, one by one, over the ship's side.

After this I slid down my rope into the water, and tied these timbers together. They formed a framework that was strong and would not sink.

On top of this framework I laid all the boards I could find.

I now had a very good raft. It was large enough to carry a great many things. All the time I was building it I was planning how to load it.

In the cabin there were three strong boxes, such as sailors use. These I emptied. Then I carried them out and let them down upon my raft.

Of all the things on board, I would need food the most. So I filled the first chest with bread, rice, cheese, and a few pieces of meat.

I found also a small bag of grain, of which I took good care. It was barley.

Then I began to look around for clothing, and found enough to do for many a day.

While I was getting these together I happened to see the carpenter's chest. It was full of tools.

It was hard work to get it on the raft. I lifted and pulled. I pulled and lifted; and at last I had it alongside of the other boxes. How tired I was!

I CARRY SOME THINGS ASHORE

IT was now past noon, and the tide was coming in. I could not stop to rest.

"I have food, I have clothing, I have tools," I said to myself. "What do I need next?"

Then I thought of the wild animals and wild men that I might meet on the shore. "How shall I protect myself from them?" I said.

In the captain's room I found two good guns with a bag of shot and a powderhorn. There were also two old swords, very rusty and dull, and a pair of big pistols.

By looking around, I found also three small kegs of powder. Two of these were dry, but the other was wet and good for nothing.

It took more than an hour to get all these safely placed on my raft. I now had quite a heavy load, and I began to wonder how I should take it to the shore.

I had no oars nor any sail for my raft. But the water was smooth, the tide was flowing in, and a gentle wind was blowing toward the land.

I loosed the rope that held the raft to the ship, and soon began my little voyage.

The tide was now so high that the dry land was much farther away than when I came out. But the raft floated smoothly along, and drew nearer and nearer to the shore.

Just as I thought myself safe, I found that I was entering a strong current which carried me into a narrow bay far from my first landing place.

There the raft stuck fast on an ugly sand bar, and was like to be tipped over. It was all I could do to keep the heavy boxes from slipping off into the water.

But the tide was still rising. Soon the raft floated free and glided slowly along again with the current.

In a short time I found that I was being carried up into a little river with high banks on each side.

With a piece of plank for an oar I pushed the raft toward the shore on my right. The water was now so shallow that I could reach the bottom.

The raft floated slowly onward until it reached a little cove into which I pushed it. The water there was quite still.

I looked around for a place to land. But the banks were steep, and if I ran one end of my raft upon the shore, the other end might sink so low as to slide all my goods into the water.

The best I could do was to wait till the tide was at its highest. Then I might push a little farther inland where the bank was somewhat lower.

This I did.

The tide rose higher and higher. At last, to my joy, the water reached the top of the bank. It covered a level spot of ground beyond.

I waited a little longer. The water on the level space was a foot deep. The tide was beginning to flow out.

With all my might I pushed the raft into this shallow place. The tide ebbed fast. Soon the raft was left high and dry on the land.

It was easy now to unload the goods and carry them to a safe place.

I LEARN THAT I AM ON AN ISLAND

THE sun was still two hours high. I was very tired after my day's work, but I could not rest. I wanted to know what sort of place I was in. I wondered whether I was on an island or on a continent.

About half a mile from the shore there was a large hill. It was steep and high and seemed to overlook all the country.

I thought that if I could get to the top of that hill I might see what kind of country I was in.

So I put one of the pistols in my belt, and one of the guns on my shoulder. I also hung the powderhorn from my neck and put a handful of small shot in my pocket.

Thus armed, I set out for the big hill.

There were but a few shrubs or trees in my way, and the walking was easy. In less than a quarter of an hour I was at my journey's end.

The sides of the hill were not rough, but they were quite steep.

Soon I was at the very top. What a grand lookout it was!

North, south, east, west, the land and the sea were spread out before me.

The sea did I say?

Yes, I was on an island, and the sea was all around.

No other land was in sight except two small islands and some great rocks that lifted themselves out of the water.

I saw that my island was not very large. Perhaps it was ten miles broad; perhaps it was twenty. I had no good idea of distances.

There was no house nor sign of life anywhere. There might be wild beasts in the woods; but I was sure that no men lived there.

The thought of being alone on a desert island made me feel very sad.

I should have been glad at that moment to see even the face of a savage.

But I dared not stay long on the hilltop. I hurried to get back to my raft before the sun should go down.

At the foot of the hill I saw a great bird sitting in a tree. I thought it to be some kind of a hawk and shot it.

The sound of the gun echoed strangely among the rocks and trees. Never before had such a sound been heard there.

I picked up the bird.

It was no hawk. It had no sharp claws nor hooked beak. Its flesh was unfit to eat, and I threw it away.

The sun had set and it was almost dark when I got back to the inlet where my raft was lying. I did not know where to go for the night, nor where to find a resting place.

But the day being gone, there was no time for thinking.

I made a kind of hut with the chests and the loose boards from the raft. Then I crept inside and lay down to rest.

For a little while I listened to every sound. At length I fell asleep and knew nothing more until broad daylight the next morning.

I HAVE A STRANGE VISITOR

THE next morning, when the tide was at its lowest I swam out to the ship again.

There were still many things on board of it that might be useful to me in my island home. I wished to save all that I could.

I climbed up the ship's side just as I had done the day before.

Before looking for anything I made another raft, just like the first one, but smaller. It was not so easy to make, for I had used up all the best planks. It was neither so large nor so strong as the first raft.

In the carpenter's shop I found three bags of nails and a grindstone. I found also a box full of little hatchets and a small barrel of musket balls.

In the captain's room I found six or seven guns, which I had overlooked before, and another keg of powder.

All these things I loaded with much care upon my raft.

Then I gathered up as many clothes as I could find; also a spare sail, a hammock, and some bedding.

The raft was now quite full. The things were not heavy, but they made a large pile.

When the tide turned for the shore, I cut loose and was soon floating homeward.

I had found a good oar in the ship. This I used as a paddle, and I had no trouble in guiding the raft to the right landing place.

I looked to see if the goods were safe which I brought over the day before.

There, on one of my chests, I saw a strange animal sitting. She looked like a wild cat.

As I went toward her, she jumped down and ran a little way. Then she stood still.

I followed. She stood very firm and looked in my face. She looked as though she had a mind to get acquainted.

I pointed my gun at her, and shouted. But she did not care for that.

I had a bit of biscuit in my pocket. This I now tossed toward her. "Take this and begone," I shouted.

Biscuits were not so many that I could well spare any. But I spared the poor animal this little bit.

It rolled quite close to her nose. She smelled of it and ate it. Then she looked up for more.

"Thank you, I have no more to give you," I said.

Whether she understood me, I do not know. But, with that, she turned and marched away.

I now set to work to get my second cargo on shore. It was no easy task, and I had to make many trips to and from the raft.

When everything was safely landed, I made me a little tent with the sail and some poles that I cut.

Then I put everything into the tent that needed to be kept dry. The empty boxes, I piled outside. They made a kind of wall around the tent, like the wall of a fort.

"This will keep the wild beasts out," I said.

By this time the day was nearly done. I spread one of the beds on the ground. I laid two loaded pistols near its head, and one of the guns by one side of it. Then I crept in and was soon fast asleep.

I FIND A GREAT STORE OF THINGS

THE next day I went to the ship again. This I kept up for more than a week.

Every day I brought a load of things to the shore.

At last there was nothing left that one pair of hands could lift. But I do believe that if the fine days had held out, I would have brought away the whole ship.

You ask how I would have done that? I would have cut it into pieces and brought one piece at a time.

The last thing that I found was a secret drawer in the cabin. In that drawer there was some money.

A part of this money was in gold pieces—"pieces of eight," we called them. The rest was in silver.

I smiled to myself when I saw this money.

"O useless stuff!" I cried. "What are you good for now? You are not worth picking up. This little old knife is worth much more. I have no manner of use for you. Lie there, where you are, and go to the bottom."

I was about to leave the cabin when I looked around again. The bright pieces were so pretty that I could not bear to leave them.

So I put them all in a strong bag and tied it around my waist like a belt.

"It will not do to throw good money away," I said.

When I went up on deck the wind was blowing hard. Dark clouds were beginning to cover the sky. The waves were rolling high. A storm was coming.

I saw that it was time for me to hurry back to the shore.

I let myself down into the water and began to swim. The sea was rough. The money was heavy. It was all I could do to reach the land.

I hastened home to my little tent. The storm had already begun.

I BUILD ME A CASTLE

 I LAY down on my bed, with my money and other precious things close at hand.

All night long the wind blew and the rain poured.

Early in the morning I arose and looked out toward the sea.

The waves were rolling very high.

The ship was gone. The sea had swallowed it up.

As I could make no more visits to the ship, I now began to think of other things.

I was still afraid lest there were savage beasts on the island.

Savage men, too, might come that way.

If any of these should find me, how could I protect myself from them?

I must have a stronger house to live in. I must build me a little fort or castle.

The place I was in was flat and wet. My tent was on open ground and could be plainly seen from a distance. There was no fresh water near it.

I must find a better place than this for my castle.

A little way from the shore there was a rocky hill. I went to look at it.

Halfway up the hill there was a large level place, with a great rock rising behind it like the side of a house.

I climbed up to the level place. There was but one way to go, and that was by a steep and winding path.

I found the place much larger than I thought. It was more than a hundred yards long and almost half as broad.

It was, indeed, a green field, or plain, with a steep cliff rising up behind it. You must think of it as a great shelf half way up the side of the hill.

"Here," I said to myself, "is the place for my castle."

It was no easy thing to carry all my goods up the steep path to this level plain. I worked hard for many days; but, then, there was nothing else to do, and I must needs keep busy.

At one place on the side of the great rock there was a break, or opening, like the door to a cave. But there was no cave there.

Just in front of this break I began to build my castle. First, I drew a half circle upon the ground, with the opening at the center. The space which it inclosed was about thirty feet across.

In this half circle I set up two rows of strong stakes, driving them deep into the ground.

The rows were not more than six inches apart. The stakes were about two inches apart and as high as my head.

Then between and around these stakes I laid the great ropes that I had brought from the ship. Among these I twined the slender branches of trees and long grapevines that I found in the woods.

When all was finished I had a wall nearly six feet high. It was so strong that nothing could break through it.

I made no door in the wall. The only way in which to get into the yard behind it was by going over the top. This was done by climbing a short ladder which I could lift up after me, and then let down again.

How safe I felt now, as I stood inside of my castle wall!

Over this wall I next carried all my riches, food, my tools, my boxes of clothing. Then, right against the great rock, I made me a large tent to shelter me from the rain.

Into this tent I brought everything that would be spoiled by getting wet. In the middle of it I swung the hammock that I had brought from the ship. For you must remember that I was a sailor, and I could sleep better in a hammock than on a bed.

The hollow place in the rock was just as I hoped. It was, indeed, a large cleft or crack, filled only with earth and small stones.

With such tools as I had I began to dig the earth and stones away. I carried them out through my tent and piled them up along the inside of my wall.

In a few days I had made quite a cave which would serve very well as a cellar to my castle.

I called the cave my kitchen; but when I began my cooking I found it best to do most of that work outside.

In bad weather, however, the kitchen was an excellent place to live in.

I GO A-HUNTING

WEEKS and weeks passed before my castle was finished.

I did not work at it all the time. Almost every day I went out with my gun to see what I could find.

The very first day I saw a flock of goats. How glad I was!

But they were very shy and very swift. As soon as they saw me they ran away in great fright.

After that, I saw them nearly every day. But it was hard to get near them.

One morning I saw an old goat feeding in the valley with a kid by her side. I crept along among the rocks in such a way that she did not see me.

When I was close enough, I raised my gun and fired. The mother goat fell, being killed at once by the shot.

It was a cruel deed, and I felt indeed sorry for the poor beast. But how else should I find food for myself in that lonely place?

The kid did not run away. It stood quite still by its mother's side. When I picked up the old goat and carried her to my castle, the little one followed me.

I lifted it over the wall. I thought I would tame it, and keep it as a pet.

But it would not eat. I could do no better than kill it and use it for my own food.

The flesh of these two goats lasted me a long time; for I did not eat much meat, and I still had many of the biscuits that I had saved from the ship.

About a month later I shot at a young goat and lamed it. I caught it and carried it home, dressed its wounded leg, and fed it.

Its leg was soon as well and as strong as ever. The little animal became quite tame and followed me everywhere I went.

I thought how fine it would be if I could have a whole flock of such creatures. Then I would be sure of food when my powder and shot were gone.

I KEEP MYSELF BUSY

AMONG the things that I brought from the ship there were several which I have not told you about. I will name them now.

First I got from the captain's desk some pens, ink, and paper. These were afterward a great comfort to me, as you shall learn.

There were some charts and compasses, and three or four books on navigation. These I threw in a corner, for I did not think I should ever need them.

Among my own things there were three very old Bibles, which I had bought in England and had packed with my clothing.

And I must not forget the dog and two cats that came to shore with me. I carried both the cats on my raft with my first cargo.

As for the dog, he jumped off the wreck and swam to the shore. He was my best friend for a long time. He followed me everywhere. He would run and fetch things to me as I bade him. I wanted him to talk to me, but this he could not do.

As for my pens, ink, and paper, I took the greatest care of them. As long as my ink lasted, I wrote down everything that happened to me.

But when that was gone, I could write no more for I did not know how to make ink.

I soon found that I needed many things to make me comfortable.

First, I wanted a chair and a table; for without them I must live like a savage.

So I set to work. I had never handled a tool in my life. But I had a saw, an ax, and several hatchets; and I soon learned to use them all.

If I wanted a board, I had to chop down a tree. From the trunk of the tree I cut a log of the length that my board was to be. Then I split the log and hewed it flat till it was as thin as a board.

All this took time and much hard work. But I had nothing else to do.

I made the table and chair out of short pieces of board I had brought from the ship.

Of the large boards which I hewed from trees, I made some wide shelves along the side of my cave or kitchen.

On these shelves I laid my tools, nails, and other things.

I had a place for everything, and kept everything in its place.

My cave looked like some stores you have seen where a little of everything is kept for sale.

From time to time I made many useful things.

From a piece of hard wood that I cut in the forest I made a spade to dig with. The handle I shaped just like the handles you buy at the stores. But the shovel part was of wood and would not last long.

While I was digging my cave, I found it very hard work to carry the earth and small stones away. I needed a wheelbarrow very much.

I could make the frame part of this, but I did not know how to make the wheel. I worked four days at it, and then had to give it up.

At last I made me a kind of hod, like that which masons use. It was better than a basket and almost as good as a wheelbarrow.

I HAVE A GREAT FRIGHT

THE very next day after my cave was finished a frightful thing happened. I came near losing everything and my own life as well.

I will tell you about it.

I was busy behind my tent when I heard a fearful noise above my head. Before I could look up, a great load of earth and stones came tumbling down.

It was a wonder that I was not buried alive. I was scared, for I thought the whole top of the cave was falling in.

I ran out and climbed over my wall. The great rock behind my castle seemed to be shaking. Stones and earth were rolling down its side.

"An earthquake! an earthquake!" I cried.

The ground shook. A tall rock that stood between me and the seashore toppled over and fell. The noise was the most frightful I ever heard.

There were three shocks about eight minutes apart. The strongest building you ever saw would have been overturned.

I was so frightened that I did not know what to do. I sat on the ground and could not move. I could only cry, over and over again, "Lord, have mercy on me!"

After the third shock was over I began to grow braver. But still I sat on the ground, wondering what would come next.

All at once the sky was overcast. Dark clouds rolled over the sea. The wind began to blow. A dreadful hurricane was at hand.

The sea was covered with foam. The waves were mountain high. On the shore, trees were torn up by the roots. If my tent had not been well sheltered behind the great rock, it would have been carried away.

The hurricane lasted fully three hours. Then the rain began to pour down.

All this time I sat on the ground outside, too much frightened to go back into my castle.

Toward night the rain slackened, and I ventured over my wall. The tent was half beaten down. So I crept through into the cave. I was half afraid that even it would tumble down on my head.

I EXPLORE MY ISLAND

IT rained all that night. But in the cave everything was warm and dry, and little by little I lost my fear.

The earthquake and the hurricane had done great damage to my castle. I had to work hard for many days to put things to rights again.

I had now been on the island about ten months. In all that time I had seen only a small part of it .

One morning I set out with my gun on my shoulder for a long walk.

I went up the little river where I had first landed with my rafts. I found that it was a very short river. After about two miles, the tide did not flow any higher; and above that, the stream was only a little brook of fresh water.

Along the brook there were pleasant meadows, covered with high grass.

In the dryer parts of these meadows I found tobacco growing wild.

I looked for the roots of a plant which the Indians use instead of bread, but could find none.

In one place, however, I saw many tall sugar canes and some fair-looking plants of a kind that was strange to me.

As I went back to my castle I wondered how I could learn something useful about the many objects I had seen. But I had never taken much thought about such things, and now I had but little chance to learn.

The next day I went up the same way, but much farther.

Beyond the meadows I came to some beautiful woods.

Here I found several different kinds of fruits. There were grapevines covering the trees, and huge clusters of ripe grapes were hanging from them.

I was very glad of this. I made up my mind to come another day and gather some of this fruit. I would dry the grapes in the sun, and have some raisins.

Night came on while I was still in the woods, and I could not do better than stay there till morning. So I climbed into a tree and slept there quite well.

It was the first night that I had spent away from home.

The next day I went on through the woods for nearly four miles.

At last I came to an open space where the land sloped to the west. The country was so fresh and green that it looked like a big garden.

I went down into a pleasant valley where there were many beautiful trees. There I found oranges, lemons, limes, and citrons, besides many grapes.

I loaded myself with fruit and started homeward. "I must come again and bring a sack," I said.

It was three days before I reached my castle. By that time the fruit had lost all its flavor.

The next day I went back to the same valley. I carried two small sacks to bring home my harvest.

But I found many of the grapevines torn down. The fruit was scattered on the ground. Some had been eaten. Some had been trodden to pieces.

A wild animal had been there. Perhaps it was a goat, perhaps it was a larger beast. Perhaps several animals had done the mischief.

I GET READY FOR WINTER

I WAS so much pleased with the valley I had discovered that I spent much of my time there.

At last I built me a small summer house close by a grove of orange trees.

It was but little more than a bower, made of the branches of trees.

I built a strong fence around it. This was made of two rows of tall stakes with brushwood between.

There was no gate in this fence, but only a short ladder, just as at my castle.

Here I sometimes stayed two or three nights together.

I gathered about two hundred clusters of grapes and hung them up to dry. In due time they made the finest of raisins. I took them down and carried them to my castle.

Thus little by little I gathered food for winter.

The winters there were not cold. But the rain fell every day, and often all the day.

I had just finished my bower, and was beginning to enjoy myself when the rainy season, or winter, began.

What could I do but hurry back to my castle and its dry, warm cave?

For weeks I could not stir out without getting wet. My store of food began to grow small.

One day, in spite of the rain, I went out and killed a goat. The next day I found a very large turtle among the rocks.

This was all good luck, for I had now enough to eat for many a day.

My meals were simple and plain.

For breakfast, I had a bunch of raisins and a bit of biscuit.

For dinner, I had broiled turtle. I could not have turtle soup, for I had no vessel in which to cook it.

For supper, I ate two or three turtle's eggs.

Although I was kept close indoors by the rain, I was never idle.

Every day I worked at making my cave larger. I dug far in, behind the rock, and made a fine, large room there.

Then I made another door or way out, which opened on the outside of my wall. So now I could come into the castle through the cellar, or kitchen, and without climbing the ladder.

This was much handier and easier than the other way. But it did not seem so safe. I feared now lest some wild beast might get into my house; and yet the biggest animal I had seen on the island was a goat.

Soon after this I put a roof over my whole inclosure. I took a number of long poles for rafters and laid one end of each on the wall, while the other end leaned against the rock above the cave.

These I covered with boughs of trees, long grass, and such other things as I could get. In this way I made a very good roof which turned the rain and kept everything dry.

My castle was now a very roomy place. It was quite warm and dry even in the worst of weather.

I MAKE ME A CALENDAR

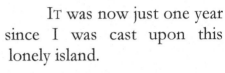

IT was now just one year since I was cast upon this lonely island.

Do you wonder how I have kept an account of the time? I will tell you.

A few days after the ship wreck it came into my mind that I should lose track of the days and the seasons. For I had neither almanac nor notebook. It would be hard always to remember the days of the week and I might even forget when it was Sunday.

So I set up a large post by my door. At the top of this post I cut in large letters these words:

I CAME ON SHORE HERE
SEPTEMBER 30, 1659.

Every morning I cut a little notch on the side of the post under these words.

49

Every seventh notch was twice as long as the rest, and this showed me that the day was Sunday.

Every thirtieth notch was longer still and broader. This showed me that a full month had gone by.

It was thus I made my calendar.

One morning I found, on counting up, that there were three hundred and sixty-five notches on the post. I knew, therefore, that it was just one year since my landing.

I kept this day as a solemn fast.

I sat in my castle and thought of the goodness of God in thus keeping me alive and safe in the midst of so many perils.

I humbled myself, and thanked him for his many mercies.

For twelve hours I tasted nothing. When, at last, the sun went down, I ate a biscuit and a bunch of grapes and went to bed.

Having now been on the island a whole year, I had learned that the seasons there were not the same as in England.

They were not to be spoken of as spring, summer, autumn, and winter. They were rather to be called the wet season and the dry season. Indeed, there were two wet seasons and two dry seasons, in the year.

I SOW SOME GRAIN

THE first wet season began about the middle of February and lasted till the middle of April.

The first dry season began about the middle of April and lasted till the middle of August.

The second wet season began about the middle of August and lasted till the middle of October.

The second dry season began about the middle of October and lasted till the middle of February.

I could not have kept track of these things easily if it had not been for my calendar.

Just before the first rainy season began I was one day rummaging among the shelves in my cave.

There I found the little bag that I had brought from the ship with some barley in it, as I have already told you.

I lifted it; it was almost empty.

I looked inside. I saw nothing there but some dust and chaff. The rats had been there, and had eaten the grains of barley.

The bag would be useful for something else. I took it outside and shook the dust and chaff upon the ground. It was a sunny place, close by the great rock.

About a month after this, I saw that something green was starting to grow at that place. I wondered what it was. It could not be grass, for the stalks were larger and stronger.

I had forgotten about the barley. But I took care that nothing should break the stalks down.

They grew fast, and were soon as high as my waist. Then I was surprised to see ten or twelve heads of green barley come out.

You cannot think how glad I was. I remembered, then, how I had shaken the bag of dust and chaff over that very spot.

But there was another surprise for me. I noticed in the wet ground a little nearer the rock some other green plants. These were not so tall as the barley stalks, and they did not seem to be the same.

I watched them for several days. Then I saw that they were stalks of rice. No doubt some grains of rice had been in the bag with the barley, and had fallen out with the dust and chaff.

You may be sure that I took good care of the grain. As soon as the barley was ripe I harvested it. There was only a handful or two; but I put it away where no rats could get to it. I wished to keep it safe and plant it again the next season.

I did the same way with the rice.

There was so little to begin with that it took a long time to grow a big crop. It was not until the fourth harvest that I could keep some of the barley for bread.

I found that the best place to plant the grain was not on the hillside, but in a moist spot not far from my summer home.

One day, as soon as the wet season was at an end, I made a visit to the country to see how my crops were growing.

There I saw something that surprised me.

You will remember the fence that I built around my summer house, or bower as I called it. It was made of two rows of tall stakes, with brush between.

Well, I now found that the stakes were still green, and that long shoots or twigs were growing from them. Some of these branches were already two or three feet long.

This pleased me very much. I cut and trained the growing branches into just such shapes as I wished.

They grew very fast, and soon the whole fence was covered with green leaves. Then I trained the long branches toward the top of a pole which I set up in the center of my bower.

In a few months the whole inclosure was covered with a green roof.

You cannot think how beautiful it was. The place was shady and cool, the pleasantest spot one could wish to have.

I did not know what kind of tree it was that grew in this wonderful way. But I cut some more stakes of the same sort and carried them home to my castle.

I set these stakes in a double row, about twenty inches outside of my first wall. In a few weeks they began to grow. They grew so fast that in two years they covered the whole space in front of my castle.

They were not only handsome to look at, but they helped to protect my castle.

I MAKE A LONG JOURNEY

I HAD long wished to see the whole of my island. So, one fine morning, I set out to travel across to the other side of it.

Of course I carried my gun with me. In my belt was my best hatchet. In my pouch I had plenty of powder and shot. In my pocket were two biscuits and a big bunch of raisins. My dog followed behind me.

I went past my summer house, or bower, and toward evening came to a fine open place close by the sea.

It was a beautiful sight. The sky was clear, the air was still. The smooth waters stretched away and away toward the setting sun.

Far in the distance I could see land. I could not tell whether it was an island or some part of the mainland of America. It was at least fifty miles away.

If it were the mainland, I felt quite sure that I would at some time or other see a ship sailing hither to it or from it. If it were an island, there might be savages on it whom it would not be safe for me to meet. But it would do no good to worry my mind about such matters.

I found this side of the island much more beautiful than that where my castle was.

Here were large, open fields, green with grass and sweet with flowers. Here, too, were fine woods, with many strange trees and vines.

I saw many green parrots among the trees, and I thought how I would catch one and teach it to talk.

After a great deal of trouble I knocked a young one down with my stick. He was a good fighter, and it was no easy matter to get him. But at last I picked him up and put him in my bag.

He was not hurt, and I carried him home. It was a long time before I could make him talk. But at last he became a great pet and would call me by my name. I shall have a funny story to tell about him after a while.

Besides parrots there were many other birds in the woods. Some of these were of kinds that I had never seen before.

In the low grounds I saw some animals that looked like rabbits. There were others that I took to be foxes, but they were not such foxes as we have in England.

I traveled very slowly around the island, for I wished to see everything. Often I did not go more than two miles in a day.

At night I sometimes slept in a tree, while my dog watched below me. Sometimes I shut myself up in a little pen made by driving tall stakes into the ground. I felt quite safe, for nothing could come near me without waking me.

Along the seashore there were thousands of turtles and a great plenty of waterfowl.

I had no trouble to find all the food I needed. Sometimes I had a roast pigeon for dinner, sometimes the juicy meat of a turtle, sometimes that of a goat. No king could have fared better.

One day my dog caught a young kid. I ran and got hold of it, and would not let him hurt it.

I had a great mind to take it home with me. So I made a collar for it, and led it along by a string which I had in my pocket.

It was quite wild and did not lead well. It gave me so much trouble that I took it to my summer house and left it there.

I then went home to my castle.

I HARVEST MY GRAIN

I CANNOT tell you how glad I was to get to my old house again and lie down in my good hammock bed.

I had been away for nearly a month.

I was so tired from my long journey that I stayed in my castle nearly a week.

While I was thus resting myself, I made a cage for my parrot which I named Poll. He was very gentle for a parrot, and soon became very fond of me.

Then I began to think of the kid that I had left in my summer bower. So I went with my dog to fetch it.

I found it where I had left it. It had eaten all the grass inside of the fence and was now very hungry.

I gave it as much as it wished, and then I tied the string to it to lead it away. But there was no need of that, for it was quite tame.

It followed me everywhere. It was very gentle and loving.

I had now a number of pets and was no longer lonesome.

My life was much happier than it had been while I was sailing the seas. I took delight in many things that I had never cared for before.

My barley and rice had grown well and in another month would be ready to be harvested.

But one day I saw that some animals had been in the field. Goats and rabbits had trampled upon the green stalks and had eaten the long blades of barley.

If things kept on this way I should soon lose my grain.

There was nothing to be done but to build a fence or hedge around the field. This was easy, for the field was not large.

I drove tall stakes into the ground all around my growing crops. These stakes were so close together that not even a rabbit could get between them.

Then I tied my dog near the gate of the little field, so that he would bark whenever any animal came near.

My grain was now safe from the beasts. It grew fast. The barley sent out large heads which soon began to ripen.

But now the birds came down in great flocks to rob me. They sat on the fence, they flew among the stalks of grain, they carried away all the ripe barley they could find.

This troubled me very much. The most of the grain was still green. But I feared that as soon as it ripened I should lose it all.

I loaded my gun and went out to the field. There I saw the thieves, sitting on the fence and watching me. I was so angry that I fired right among them and killed three.

"Now I will show you how to steal my grain!" I cried.

I put up a long pole in the center of the field, and on top of it I hung the three dead birds.

"This will I do to all that venture to come into my field," I said.

Strange to say, this ended all my troubles. Not another bird came to that place so long as my scarecrows hung there. In fact, the birds went away from that part of the island, and I did not soon see another.

I WORK UNDER MANY DIFFICULTIES

MY barley ripened and was ready to be harvested. I had neither scythe nor sickle to cut it down.

But you will remember that I had two old swords which I had found in the ship.

With one of the swords I cut off the heads of the barley and dropped them into a big basket I had made. I carried these heads into my cave and thrashed out the grain with my hands.

When all my harvesting was done, I measured the grain. I had two bushels of rice and two bushels and a half of barley.

This pleased me very much. I felt now that I should soon be able to raise grain enough for food.

Have you ever thought how many things are necessary for the making of your bread?

You have nothing to do but eat the bread after others have made it. But I had to sow, to reap, to thrash, to grind, to sift, to mix, and to bake.

To do all these I needed many tools.

I had no plow to turn up the ground. I had no spade nor shovel with which to dig it. But with great labor I made me a wooden spade, which was better than nothing.

After the ground was turned up, I sowed the seed by scattering it with my hands. But it must be covered so it would grow, and I had no harrow. I cut down the branch of a tree, and dragged it over the field. This, I think, was the way that people in old times harrowed their ground.

The third thing to be done was to build a fence around my field. After that came the reaping, the curing, the carrying home, the thrashing, the parting of the grain from the chaff, the grinding.

I needed a mill to do the grinding. I needed a sieve to sift the flour. I needed yeast and salt to mix with the dough. I needed an oven to bake it.

I had to do without the most of these things. And this made my work very slow and hard.

I was very lucky in having saved so many tools from the wreck, and for this I was indeed thankful. What a hard case I would have been in if I had saved nothing at all!

From time to time, as I felt the need of things I made a number of tools that served me very well. They were not such tools as you would buy at the store, but what did it matter?

I have already told you about the shovel which I made from a piece of hard wood. Next to the shovel I needed a pickax most of all.

Among the many things that I had saved from the wreck, I found an old crowbar. This I heated in the fire until it was almost white hot.

I then found that I could bend it quite easily. Little by little I shaped it until I had made quite a good pickax of it. Of course, it was heavy and not at all pretty. But who would look for beauty in a pickax?

I at first felt the need of some light baskets in which to carry my fruit and grain. So I began to study how baskets are made.

It was not until I had searched almost every nook on the island that I found some long slender twigs that would bend to make wicker ware. Then I spent many an hour learning how to weave these twigs together and shape them into the form of a basket.

In the end, however, I was able to make as good baskets as were ever bought in the market.

I had quite a goodly number of edge tools. Among these there were three large axes and a great store of hatchets; for you will remember that we carried hatchets to trade with the savages. I had also many knives.

But all these became very dull with use. I had saved a grindstone from the wreck, but I could not turn it and grind my tools at the same time.

I studied hard to overcome this difficulty. At last, I managed to fasten a string to the crank of the grindstone in such a way that I could turn it with my foot.

My tools were soon sharp, and I kept them so.

I BECOME A POTTER

WHEN it came to making bread, I found that I needed several vessels. In fact, I needed them in many ways.

It would be hard to make wooden vessels. Of course it was out of the question to make vessels of iron or any other metal. But why might I not make some earthen vessels?

If I could find some good clay, I felt quite sure that I could make pots strong enough to be of use.

After much trouble I found the clay. The next thing was to shape it into pots or jars.

You would have laughed to see the first things I tried to make. How ugly they were!

Some of them fell in pieces of their own weight. Some of them fell in pieces when I tried to lift them.

They were of all shapes and sizes.

After I had worked two months I had only two large jars that were fit to look at. These I used for holding my rice and barley meal.

Then I tried some smaller things, and did quite well.

I made some plates, a pitcher, and some little jars that would hold about a pint.

All these I baked in the hot sun. They kept their shape, and seemed quite hard. But of course they would not hold water or bear the heat of the fire.

One day when I was cooking my meat for dinner, I made a very hot fire. When I was done with it, I raked down the coals and poured water on it to put it out.

It so happened that one of my little earthenware jars had fallen into the fire and been broken. I had not taken it out, but had left it in the hot flames.

Now, as I was raking out the coals, I found some pieces of it and was surprised at the sight of them, for they were burned as hard as stones and as red as tiles.

"If broken pieces will burn so," said I, "why cannot a whole jar be made as hard and as red as these?"

I had never seen potters at work. I did not know how to build a kiln for firing the pots. I had never heard how earthenware is glazed.

But I made up my mind to see what could be done.

I put several pots and small jars in a pile, one upon another. I laid dry wood all over and about them, and then set it on fire.

As fast as the wood burned up, I heaped other pieces upon the fire. The hot flames roared all round the jars and pots. The red coals burned beneath them.

I kept the fire going all day. I could see the pots become red-hot through and through. The sand on the side of a little jar began to melt and run.

After that I let the fire go down, little by little. I watched it all night, for I did not wish the pots and jars to cool too quickly.

In the morning I found that I had three very good earthen pots. They were not at all pretty, but they were as hard as rocks and would hold water.

I had two fine jars also, and one of them was well glazed with the melted sand.

After this I made all the pots and jars and plates and pans that I needed. They were of all shapes and sizes.

You would have laughed to see them.

Of course I was awkward at this work. I was like a child making mud pies.

But how glad I was when I found that I had a vessel that would bear the fire! I could hardly wait to put some water in it and boil me some meat.

That night I had turtle soup and barley broth for supper.

I BUILD A BIG CANOE

WHILE I was doing these things I was always trying to think of some way to escape from the island.

True, I was living there with much comfort. I was happier than I had ever been while sailing the seas.

But I longed to see other men. I longed for home and friends.

You will remember that when I was over at the farther side of the island I had seen land in the distance. Fifty or sixty miles of water lay between me and that land. Yet I was always wishing that I could reach it.

It was a foolish wish. For there was no telling what I might find on that distant shore.

Perhaps it was a far worse place than my little island. Perhaps there were savage beasts there. Perhaps wild men lived there who would kill me and eat me.

I thought of all these things; but I was willing to risk every kind of danger rather than stay where I was.

At last I made up my mind to build a boat. It should be large enough to carry me and all that belonged to me. It should be strong enough to stand a long voyage over stormy seas.

I had seen the great canoes which Indians sometimes make of the trunks of trees. I would make one of the same kind.

In the woods I found a cedar tree which I thought was just the right thing for my canoe.

It was a huge tree. Its trunk was more than five feet through at the bottom.

I chopped and hewed many days before it fell to the ground. It took two weeks to cut a log of the right length from it.

Then I went to work on the log. I chopped and hewed and shaped the outside into the form of a canoe. With hatchet and chisel I hollowed out the inside.

For full three months I worked on that cedar log. I was both proud and glad when the canoe was finished. I had never seen so big a boat made from a single tree.

It was well shaped and handsome. More than twenty men might find room to sit in it.

But now the hardest question of all must be answered.

How was I to get my canoe into the water?

It lay not more than three hundred feet from the little river where I had first landed with my raft.

But how was I to move it three hundred feet, or even one foot? It was so heavy that I could not even roll it over.

I thought of several plans. But when I came to reckon the time and the labor, I found that even by the easiest plan it would take twenty years to get the canoe into the water.

What could I do but leave it in the woods where it lay?

How foolish I had been! Why had I not thought of the weight of the canoe before going to the labor of making it?

The wise man will always look before he leaps. I certainly had not acted wisely.

I went back to my castle, feeling sad and thoughtful.

Why should I be discontented and unhappy?

I was the master of all that I saw. I might call myself the king of the island.

I had all the comforts of life.

I had food in plenty.

I might raise shiploads of grain, but there was no market for it.

I had thousands of trees for timber and fuel, but no one wished to buy.

I counted the money which I had brought from the ship. There were above a hundred pieces of gold and silver; but of what use were they?

I would have given all for a handful of peas or beans to plant. I would have given all for a bottle of ink.

I MAKE AN UMBRELLA

As the years went by the things which I had brought from the ship were used up or worn out.

My biscuits lasted more than a year; for I ate only one cake each day.

My ink soon gave out, and then I had no more use for pens or paper.

At last my clothes were all worn out.

The weather was always warm on my island and there was little need for clothes. But I could not go without them.

It so happened that I had saved the skins of all the animals I had killed.

I stretched every skin on a framework of sticks and hung it up in the sun to dry.

In time I had a great many of these skins. Some were coarse and stiff and fit for nothing. Others were soft to the touch and very pretty to look at.

One day I took one of the finest and made me a cap of it. I left all the hair on the outside, so as to shoot off the rain.

It was not very pretty; but it was of great use, and what more did I want?

I did so well with the cap that I thought I would try something else. So, after a great deal of trouble, I made me a whole suit.

I made me a waistcoat and a pair of knee breeches. I wanted them to keep me cool rather than warm. So I made them quite loose.

You would have laughed to see them. They were funny things, I tell you. But when I went out in the rain, they kept me dry.

This, I think, put me in mind of an umbrella.

I had seen umbrellas in Brazil, although they were not yet common in England. They were of much use in the summer when the sun shone hot.

I thought that if they were good in Brazil, they would be still better here, where the sun was much hotter.

So I set about the making of one.

I took great pains with it, and it was a long time before it pleased me at all.

I could make it spread, but it did not let down. And what would be the use of an umbrella that could not be folded?

I do not know how many weeks I spent at this work. It was play work rather than anything else, and I picked it up only at odd times.

At last I had an umbrella that opened and shut just as an umbrella should.

I covered it with skins, with the hair on the outside. In the rain it was as good as a shed. In the sun it made a pleasant shade.

I could now go out in all kinds of weather. I need not care whether the rain fell or the sun shone.

For the next five years I lived very quietly. I kept always busy and did not allow myself to feel lonely.

I divided each day into parts according to my several duties.

After reading in my Bible, it was my custom to spend about three hours every morning in search of food. Through the heat of the day, I busied myself in the shade of my castle or bower.

In the evening, when the sun was low, I worked in my fields. But sometimes I went to work very early in the morning and left my hunting until the afternoon.

I HAVE A PERILOUS
ADVENTURE

I HAD never given up the idea of having a canoe.

My first trial, as you have seen, was a failure. I had made too big a boat, and I had made it too far from the water. I could do better another time.

One day after I had harvested my grain, I set to work.

There was no tree near the river that was fit for a canoe. But I found a fine one nearly half a mile away.

Before I began to chop the tree, I made all my plans for taking the canoe to the water.

I worked now with a will, for I felt sure that I would succeed.

In a few weeks the little vessel was finished. It was a very pretty canoe, and large enough for only two or three persons.

Small as it was, it was quite heavy. For you must remember that it was a part of the tree, hollowed out and shaped like a boat. It was as much as I could do to lift one end of it.

How should I ever get it to the river?

I have already told you that I had made plans for this.

Through the soft ground between the river and the canoe I dug a big ditch. It was four feet deep and six feet wide and nearly half a mile long.

I worked at this ditch for nearly two years. When it was done and filled with water from the river, I slid my canoe into it. It floated, as I knew it would.

As I pushed it along to the end of the great ditch and out into the river, it looked very small. I could never hope to make a long voyage in it!

But I could sail round the island, and make little journeys close to the shore.

Before starting out, I put up a mast in the prow of the canoe and made a sail for it of a piece of the ship's sail that I had kept with great care.

Then at each end of the little vessel I made lockers or small boxes, in which I put a supply of food and other things that I would need on my voyage.

On the inside of the vessel I cut a little, long, hollow place or shelf where I could lay my gun; and above this I tacked a long flap of goatskin to hang down over it and keep it dry.

In the stern I set up my umbrella, so that it would keep the hot sun off of me while I was steering the canoe.

Then every day I made short trips down the river to the sea and back again. Sometimes, when the wind was fair, I sailed a little way out; but I was afraid to go far.

At last I made up my mind for a voyage around the island.

I filled my lockers with food. In one I put two dozen barley cakes and a pot full of parched rice. In the other I stored the hind quarters of a goat.

I also put in powder and shot enough to kill as much game as I would need.

On a day in November I set sail on my voyage. It proved to be a harder voyage than I had bargained for.

In the first place, there were so many rocks along the shore that I sometimes had to sail for miles out into the sea to get around them.

Then, when I was on the farther side of the island, I struck a furious current of water that was pouring round a point of land like the sluice of a mill.

I could do nothing in such a current. My canoe was whirled along like a leaf in a whirlwind. The sail was of no use. The little vessel spun round and round in the eddies and was carried far out to sea.

I gave myself up for lost. I was so far out that I could hardly see the low shores of my island.

Suddenly I noticed that the canoe was only a little way from the edge of the current. Just beyond it the water was quite calm and smooth.

I took up my paddle again and paddled with all my might. With great joy I soon found myself floating in quiet water.

The wind was fair for the shore, and I set my sail again. The canoe sped swiftly back toward the island.

I saw then that I was sailing midway between two strong currents. If I should be caught in either, I would again be carried out to sea.

I needed all the skill I had to steer the canoe aright. At last, when the sun was almost down, I brought it into a quiet little cove where the shore was green with grass.

I AM ALARMED BY A VOICE

As soon as I touched the land, I fell upon my knees and gave God thanks for bringing me safe out of so great danger.

I made the canoe fast to a rock by the shore, and lay down on the grass.

I was so tired that I soon fell asleep and did not waken once until the next morning.

I went up a little hill close by the shore, and looked around to see what part of the island I was in.

To my right I saw some well-known trees which I had visited when I was exploring the island. Then I knew that I was only a little way from my summer house and that I could reach it easily by walking.

I was sick of the sea, and I thought that nothing would be so pleasant as a few days in my quiet bower.

So, with my umbrella over my head, I started across the country. It was a hot day, and I walked slowly.

I stopped often to rest, and did not reach my summer house until it was growing dark.

I saw that everything was standing just as I had left it; for I always kept it in good order.

As soon as I got over the fence, I sat down to rest; and I was so tired that I fell asleep.

Then, all at once in the darkness, I heard a voice calling me, "Robin, Robin, Robin Crusoe!"

I was so full of sleep that I did not wake up at once. But between sleeping and waking I could hear somebody saying, "Robin Crusoe, Robin Crusoe!"

I wondered who it could be, but I was still more than half asleep.

Then the voice screamed in my ear, "ROBIN CRUSOE!"

I sprang to my feet. I was frightened almost out of my wits. Who in the world could be speaking my name in that place?

No sooner were my eyes well open than I saw in the dim light of the moon my Poll Parrot sitting on a post quite close to my shoulder.

"Poor Robin Crusoe," he said. "Poor Robin Crusoe."

He was looking down at me as though in pity.

He was but repeating the words I had taught him. I knew that he was glad to see me, as I also was glad to see him.

I let him sit on my thumb as he often did at home. He rubbed his bill on my face and kept saying: "Poor Robin Crusoe! Where are you? Where have you been?" and other words that he knew.

I wondered how the bird had come to this place, for I had left him at the castle. I asked him, "Why are you here, Poll?"

But he answered me only by saying: "Poor Robin Crusoe! Where have you been?"

I surely believe that the bird loved me.

In the morning I carried him with me back to my castle.

As for the canoe, I would gladly have brought it back to its place in the little river. But I was afraid of being caught again in the furious currents; and so I left it in the safe cove on the other side of the island.

I AM HAPPY AS A KING

I HAD now had adventures enough for a time, and I felt very happy to be at home with my goats and other pets.

A few years before, I had started with keeping three kids that I had caught. Now I had a herd of three and forty goats, some of them young, some old.

I kept them in five little fields that I had fenced, at the foot of my castle hill. I never had any lack of meat and I had plenty of milk, too.

Indeed, I had gone so far as to set up a little dairy, and sometimes my goats gave me a gallon or two of milk in a day.

Before coming to the island I had never milked a cow, much less a goat. I had never seen butter made, or even cheese. But I learned how to do everything of the kind. And now I had more butter and cheese than I could eat.

After dinner it was my custom to go out for a stroll. How proud I was of my little kingdom!

If you had seen me then, you would not have laughed. You would have been frightened. For a stranger-looking fellow you never saw.

Be pleased to take a picture of me.

On my head was a big cap made of goatskin. It was very tall and without shape. A flap hung down from the back of it to keep the rain off my neck.

I wore a short jacket of goatskin and a pair of knee breeches of the same.

I had neither stockings nor shoes. But I wore around my legs and feet some queer things that I called buskins. They were made of goatskin, too, and were of great use when walking among briers or stones.

Around my waist I had a broad belt of rawhide. I had no need of sword or dagger; and so I carried in this belt a little saw and a hatchet.

Another belt, which hung over my shoulder, held my powderhorn and shot pouch.

On my back was slung a basket. On my shoulder was my gun. Above my head I carried my great clumsy, ugly umbrella.

My face was as dark as mahogany. It was tanned by the sun and browned by the hot winds.

My beard was at one time a yard long. But I soon grew tired of it and cut it pretty short. Yet even then it looked grizzly enough, I assure you.

It is not a very handsome picture, is it?

But do not blame me. I dressed as well as I could. I kept myself clean. I tried to be worthy of respect, even though no one saw me.

I looked over my little kingdom and was proud and happy.

You would have laughed to see me and my family when dinner time came.

First there was myself, Robinson Crusoe, king of the island. I was the lord of everything I could see.

Then, like a king, I dined alone, with my servants looking on.

No one was allowed to talk to me but Poll Parrot, who sat on the back of my chair and waited for what I would give him.

My dog was now so old and feeble that he could hardly stir. He sat always at my right hand and wagged his tail if I did but snap my finger.

My two cats waited, one on each side of the table, to see what I would give them.

These two cats were not the same that I had brought from the ship. Those were dead, long ago, of old age. But they had left many kittens.

Indeed, there had come to be so many cats that I was forced to drive them away. All but these two had gone into the woods and become very wild.

I LEARN TO BAKE AND AM PROSPEROUS

I HAVE already told you about farming, and of the difficulties under which I did my work. The thing which I wished to do most of all was to make good bread.

I tried many plans, but it was several years before I could think of myself as a really good baker.

My barley was very fine. The grains were large and smooth. When boiled a long time with a bit of goat's meat, they made good food.

But they did not take the place of bread. Before bread could be made, the grains of barley must be ground into meal.

I tried pounding them with a stone. But that was slow work. The stone crumbled into sand. My meal was worth nothing.

87

I looked all over the island for a harder stone. All were alike.

So at last I cut a large block of very hard wood. I rounded it on the outside with my hatchet. Then, partly by chopping, partly by burning, I made a hollow place in the end of it.

Out of a piece of ironwood I made a heavy pestle or beater.

I had now a very good little mill. In a short time I had crushed enough barley to make meal for a large loaf.

It was easy to make the dough. I had only to mix the meal with water and knead it with my hands. I must not think of yeast to make the dough light.

The baking part was the main thing, and the hardest to learn.

At first I put my biscuits of dough in the hot ashes and left them there till they were baked. But I did not like these ash cakes very well.

Then I tried another plan.

I made two large earthen vessels. They were broad and shallow. Each was about two feet across and not more than nine inches deep.

These I burned in the fire till they were as hard as rocks and as red as tiles.

I made also a hearth before my fireplace, and paved it with some square tiles of my own making. But, perhaps I ought not to call them square.

The hearth, when finished, was quite level and smooth. It was as pretty as I could have wished.

Next I built a great fire of hard wood. When the wood had burned down, I raked the hot coals out upon my hearth. I left them there till the hearth was hot through and through.

My loaves of dough were all ready. I swept the hearth clean and then put the loaves down upon the hottest part of it.

Over each loaf I put one of the large earthen vessels I had made. Then I heaped hot coals on the top of the vessel and all round the sides of it.

In a short time I lifted the vessels and took out my loaves. They were baked as well as the best oven in the world could have baked them.

By trying and trying again, I at last learned to bake almost everything I wanted. I baked cakes and rice pudding fit for a king. But I did not care for pies.

I now felt quite contented and prosperous. For did I not have everything that I needed?

I had two homes on the island. I called them my plantations.

The first of these was my strong castle under the rock. I had enlarged it until my cave contained many rooms, one opening into another.

The largest and driest of these was my storeroom. Here I kept the largest of my earthen pots. Here also were fourteen or fifteen big baskets, all filled with grain.

My sitting room was not large, but it was made for comfort.

As for the wall in front of the castle, it was a wonderful thing. The long stakes which I had driven down had all taken root. They had grown like trees, and were now so big and so thick with branches that it was hard to see between them.

No one passing by would ever think there was a house behind this matted row of trees.

Near this dwelling of mine, but a little farther within the land, were my two barley fields. These I cultivated with care, and from them I reaped a good harvest. As often as I felt the need of more barley I made my fields larger.

Farther away was what I called my country seat. There was my pleasant summer house or bower, where I liked to go for rest.

In the middle of my bower I had my tent always set. It was made of a piece of sail spread over some poles.

Under the tent I had made a soft couch with the skins of animals and a blanket thrown over them. Here, when the weather was fair, I often slept at night.

A little way from the bower was the field in which I kept my cattle—that is to say, my goats.

I had taken great pains to fence and inclose this field. I was so fearful, lest the goats should break out, that I worked many a day planting a hedge all around. The hedge grew to be very tall and was as strong as a wall.

On the shore of the sea, some distance beyond my summer house, was the little inlet where I had laid up my canoe.

I SEE SOMETHING IN THE SAND

WHEN the weather was fine I often went over to the other side of the island to look at my canoe.

Sometimes I spent several days at my summer house. Then, going over to where the canoe was kept, I took short sails along the shore. These little voyages gave me a great deal of pleasure.

One morning as I was going to the canoe a strange thing happened.

I was walking slowly along and looking down, and what do you think I saw?

I saw the print of a man's naked foot in the sand.

The sight made me cold all over.

I stood like one that had seen a ghost. I looked around. I listened. I trembled.

I went to the top of a little hill to look farther. Then I walked up the shore and down the shore. I saw no other tracks.

I went back to make sure that I was not dreaming. Yes, there in the sand was the print of man's foot. It showed the toes, the heel, and the sole of the foot. I was not dreaming.

My mind was filled with a thousand thoughts and questions. Where was the man who made that track? Who was he? How did he get there?

I was so frightened that I did not go to the canoe. I turned back and went to my castle as fast as I could.

Whether I went over by the ladder or through the hole in the rock, I do not know. But I shut myself up as quickly as I could and began to get ready to defend myself.

That night I could not sleep. I lay in my hammock, and thought and thought.

The track must have been made by an Indian or some other wild savage. This savage had come perhaps from the land that I had seen far across the sea.

Perhaps he had come to the island alone. Perhaps he had come with many others of his kind. But where was he now?

I was so much afraid that I did not stir out of my castle for three days and nights. I was almost starved, for I had only two or three barley cakes in my kitchen.

Little by little I became brave enough to go out again. I crept softly down to my fields to milk the goats. Poor things! They were glad enough to see me.

But every sound made me start and look around. I fancied that I saw a savage behind every tree. I lived for days like some hunted thing that trembles at its own shadow.

And all because I had seen the print of a foot in the sand!

Little by little I grew bolder, and I made up my mind to strengthen my castle. If savage Indians should indeed come and find me, I would be ready for them.

So I carried out earth and small stones, and piled them up against the castle wall till it was ten feet thick. I have already told you how strong it was at first, and how I had made a dense hedge of trees on the outside. It was now so strong that nothing could break through it.

Through the wall at certain places I made five holes large enough for a man's arm to reach in. In each of these holes I planted a gun; for you will remember that I brought several from the ship.

Each one of these guns was fitted in a frame that could be drawn back and forth. They worked so well in their places that I could shoot off all five of them in less than two minutes.

Many a weary month did I work before I had my wall to my notion. But at last it was finished.

The hedge that was before it grew up so thick and high that no man nor animal could see through it. If you had seen it, you would not have dreamed there was anything inside of it, much less a house.

For two years I lived in fear. All that I did was to make my home stronger and safer.

Far in the woods I built a large pen of logs and stakes. Around it I planted a hedge like that in front of the castle. Then I put a dozen young goats into it, to feed upon the grass and grow.

If savages should come, and if they should kill the other goats, they could not find these; for they were too well hidden in the deep woods.

All these things I did because I had seen the print of a man's foot in the sand.

I AM AGAIN ALARMED

FIVE or six years had passed, and not another footprint had I seen.

I had gotten over my great fright, and yet I was not so bold as I had been. Any sudden sound would make me start and look around.

I thought that if savage men had been on the island once, they were quite likely to come again. So I kept on the lookout for them all the time.

My flock of goats had now grown to be very large, and I needed another field. I wished to put some of them in a hidden spot where the savages, if they did come, would not find them.

I had already a small flock in one such spot, as I have told you. But now I wished to have another.

In looking for the right kind of place, I went all over the island. I even went far out on a rocky point beyond the place where I kept my canoe.

As I was standing on a rock and looking out to sea, I thought I saw a boat in the distance. It was only a little speck on the water, and it seemed to rise and fall with the waves. It could not be a rock.

I looked at it till my eyes could look no more. I had saved a spyglass out of the ship; but, as luck would have it, I had left it at home. How I wished for it then!

Whether I really saw a boat or not, I do not know. But as I walked back along the shore, I made up my mind never to go out again without my spyglass.

I walked slowly along, thinking of what I had seen. All at once I came upon that which made my heart stand still.

On the sandy, sloping beach of a pleasant little harbor I saw not only one footprint, but hundreds of them.

I stood still, afraid to move.

But the footprints were not all. The beach at one place was covered with bones and bits of flesh, as in a slaughter house. Some of the bones were quite fresh; some had been charred with fire.

"Here the savages have been holding a feast," I said to myself.

A little farther on I saw that a pit had been dug in the sand, and here they had had their fire. The ashes were still warm.

I wondered what kind of a feast these wild men had been having. There were savages on the mainland who were said to kill and eat the captives whom they took in war. Cannibals, they were called.

Could this have been a feast of cannibals? And were these the bones and flesh of human beings?

I trembled as I thought of it.

I turned and ran from the place as fast as I could.

I ran until I could go no farther. My breath came fast. I sank down upon the ground.

When I had rested a little while, I looked around and found that I was not very far from my castle. All around me was peaceful and still. I was surely safe from harm.

With tears in my eyes I knelt down and gave thanks to God. I thanked him that he had kept me alive and safe through so many years. I thanked him that I had been cast on the side of the island which was never visited by savages. I thanked him for all the comforts and blessings that were mine.

Then I arose and went home to my castle.

As I sat before my door that evening, I thought the whole matter over, and felt much easier in my mind.

I had been on the island eighteen years before I saw the first footprint. I had been there twenty-three years before I saw any other signs of savages. It was likely that many more years would pass before any harm should come to me.

With these thoughts I lay down in my hammock and slept without fear.

But it was a long time before I went again to the farther shore of the island. I did not even go to look after my canoe.

The days went quietly by. I kept quite close to my castle, and busied myself with my goats and my grain.

I was always on my guard, and never stepped out of doors without first looking around me.

I MAKE A SURPRISING DISCOVERY

ONCE every week I went into the woods to see the flock of goats that I had hidden there.

I always carried my gun, but since my last great fright I did not dare to fire it off. I was afraid even to drive a nail or chop a stick of wood, lest some savages might be near enough to hear the sound.

I was afraid to build a fire at my castle, lest the smoke should be seen.

At last I carried some of my pots and kettles to my hidden field in the woods. I could do my cooking there much more safely than at my castle.

Hardly had I put things in order there when I found something that made me very glad. What do you suppose it was?

It was a cave—a real cave. The door into it was through a little hollow place at the bottom of a great rock. It was so well hidden that no one could have found it even by looking for it.

Shall I tell you how I came upon it?

I was afraid to make a smoke near my house, and yet I could not live without cooking meat. I tried all kinds of dry wood, and yet there was always some smoke. Then I thought I would try charcoal. But I must first make the charcoal.

I found a place in the darkest part of the woods where the smoke would hardly rise to the tops of the trees. There I built my charcoal pit.

This was done in the following way:—

First, I cleared off a round space about ten feet in diameter. Here I dug out the earth till I made a pit about a foot deep. Then I cut a cord or more of wood and piled it up in this space. I piled it up until it was almost as high as my shoulders. I covered it a foot deep with earth and turf, leaving a small open place at the bottom.

When this was done, I set fire to the wood through the hole in the bottom. It burned slowly. The wood became charcoal.

One day, while cutting wood for my charcoal pit, I happened to see a hollow place in the rock close by a tree I was chopping.

It was half covered with brush. I pushed this aside and looked in. I saw a little cave just large enough for me to creep into on my hands and knees.

But, a little farther in, it was larger. It was so high that I could stand upright, and it was so wide that two men could have walked in it side by side.

It was a very dark place, and I stood still a moment till my eyes should become a little used to it.

All at once I saw something in the darkness that made me scramble out of that place much faster than I had come into it.

What do you think it was? Two big shining eyes that glowed like coals in the darkness. Whether they were the eyes of a man or of some fierce beast, I did not stop to see.

I stood a little while by the mouth of the cave and then I began to get over my fright.

What could there be in this cave that would do me harm? No man could live there in the darkness. As for any animal, I knew there was nothing fiercer on the island than one of my cats.

So, with a blazing stick for a torch, I crept back into the cave. But I had not gone three steps before I was frightened almost as much as before.

I heard a loud sigh, like that of a man in trouble. Then there were low moans, and sounds as of some one trying to speak.

I stopped short. Cold chills ran down my back. My hair seemed to stand on end. But I would not allow myself to run out again.

I pushed my little torch forward into the darkness, as far as I could. The blaze lit up the cave. And what do you suppose I saw then?

Why, nothing but a shaggy old goat that I had missed from my flock for nearly a week past.

He was stretched on the floor of the cave, and too weak to rise up. He was a very old fellow, and perhaps had gone in there to die.

I gave him some food and water, and made him as comfortable as I could. But he was too far gone to live long.

I found that, although I could stand up in the cave, it was very small. It was only a hole in the rocks, and was neither round nor square.

But at the end of this little chamber there seemed to be a passage that led farther in. This passage was very narrow and dark, and as my torch had burned out, I did not try to follow it.

I went back to my wood chopping.

I EXPLORE MY CAVE
FURTHER

THE next day I brought out with me six big candles.

For you must know that I was a candle maker as well as a baker. Indeed, I made very good candles of goats' tallow, using some bits of old ropes for the wicks.

As I have just said, I took six candles with me, for I had made up my mind to learn more about the cave I had found.

I lit two of the candles, and went in. The poor old goat was dead, and it was no easy work to dig a hole right there and bury him.

After this unpleasant task was done, I went into the back part of the cave. The flame of the candles lighted up the darkness, and I could see quite plainly.

The narrow passage of which I have told you was no less than thirty feet long. In one place it was so low that I had to creep through on all fours.

But no sooner was I through this low place than I found myself in a splendid chamber. It was large enough to shelter a hundred men.

Indeed, it seemed like the great hall of some old English castle. I had never seen anything so grand.

The roof was at least twenty feet high. The light from my two candles shone upon the walls and made it look as though covered with thousands of bright stars.

Whether these were diamonds, or gold, or some other precious things, I did not know, and in fact I never learned.

The floor was dry and level. It was covered with white sand, which was very clean.

I was delighted. No better or safer storehouse could I have wished.

When I had looked at the room on every side and found that it was really the end of the cave, I went out and hurried back to my castle.

I found that I still had about sixty pounds of powder. This was the first thing that I carried to my new cavern. I took thither also the lead that I had for making bullets and small shot.

I felt now like one of the wonderful elves that you read about. They live, as you know, in rocks and in caves where none can get at them; and they have hidden treasures of gold and precious stones.

What if a hundred savages should hunt me? They could not come near me here. I was safe from all foes.

I fitted the cave up with whatever was needed to make it comfortable.

If the worst came to the worst, I meant to live there. And yet I did not wish to be obliged to do this.

When everything was safe and snug, I laid some green branches over the entrance and went back to my castle.

I was very glad when I sat down in my old kitchen again. For, after all, no other place was so much like home.

I had now been twenty-three years on this island. If it had not been for fear of savages, I would have been the happiest man in the world.

During all those years I had been very busy. I did not work all the time, as you know, but I amused myself in various ways.

I spent much time with Poll, the parrot. He soon learned to talk so well that it was a pleasure to hear him.

My dog had been my best friend and companion. He lived for sixteen years, and then died of old age.

As for my cats, the woods were full of them. All ran wild except the two that I kept in my castle. These were good mousers and fine pets.

I had also several tame fowls. These I had caught near the seashore when they were young. I cut their wing feathers short and taught them to eat from my hand.

I never knew what kind of birds they were, but they were large, almost as large as chickens. They lived among the hedge trees in front of my castle.

They made their nests there and kept me well supplied with eggs. I did not need to keep any other poultry.

Thus I lived very pleasantly in my island home. I would have been content to live there always if I could have felt safe from savages.

I SEE SAVAGES

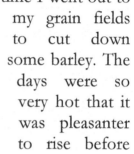 EARLY one morning in harvest time I went out to my grain fields to cut down some barley. The days were so very hot that it was pleasanter to rise before daylight and do the heavier part of my work before the sun was high.

On this morning of which I am telling you, I started out while it was still quite dark. I had been to the fields so often that I could have found the way with my eyes shut.

As I went along, I was surprised to see a light far over toward my side of the island. I stopped and looked. It was plainly the light of a blazing fire.

Who could have built a fire there?

Surely none but savages.

I was so much surprised that I stood still and wondered.

What if those savages should find my grain fields?

They would know at once that somebody had planted them, and they would never rest till they should find me.

I could now see the blaze quite plainly. As the day dawned, I could also see the smoke rising above the trees. The fire was not more than two miles away.

I hurried back to my castle as fast as I could run. I made everything on the outside of it look as wild as possible.

I climbed over the wall and pulled up the ladder after me.

I loaded all my cannon, as I called the guns, that I had placed in the wall. I put everything in order for a siege.

Then I waited to see if any enemy would come near.

Two hours, three hours passed, and there was no sight nor sound that was at all uncommon. I began to wonder if, after all, the fire had been kindled by some accident and not by strange men.

At last I could wait no longer. I set up my ladder against the side of the rock and climbed up to a flat place above my castle. I pulled the ladder up after me and then mounted to another landing. I pulled it up a second time, and it now reached to the top of the great rock.

Here was the place I called my lookout.

Very carefully I climbed up. I laid myself down upon the rock and through my spyglass looked over toward the place where I had seen the fire.

I could still see the smoke. Yes, and I could see some naked savages sitting around a small fire.

I counted them, and made out that there were no fewer than nine of the wretches.

They surely did not need a fire to warm themselves by, for the day was very hot. No doubt they were cooking something. Perhaps they were cannibals and were getting ready for one of their horrible feasts.

On the beach not far from them I saw the two canoes in which they had arrived.

The tide was now at its lowest. When it returned and floated the canoes, they would probably go away.

This thought made me feel much easier, for I was sure they would not wander far inland.

I waited and watched till the tide was again at the flood.

Then I saw them all get into the boats and paddle away. They seemed to be going around to the other side of the island.

I could now breathe freely again. As soon as they were well gone, I armed myself and hurried across the land to see if I could get another sight of them.

I carried two guns on my shoulder, two pistols in my belt, and a big sword at my side. You would have been frightened, had you seen me.

It was a long, hard walk. But by and by I came to the hill that overlooked the farther shore of the island.

This I climbed. I scanned sea and land with my spyglass.

Yes, there were the two canoes coming slowly around the coast.

But what was my surprise to see three other boats put off from a cove near by and hasten around to meet them!

It seemed, then, that another party of savages had been feasting at the very spot where I had seen the first footprint in the sand.

I watched the canoes until all five were far out to sea, on their way to the low-lying shore in the distant west.

Then I went down to the place where the savages had been feasting.

What a dreadful sight met my eyes! The sand was covered with blood and bones. No doubt some poor captive had been killed there and eaten.

I made up my mind that if any other savages should ever come to my island for such a feast, I would not let them enjoy it.

I gathered up the bones and buried them in the sand. Then I went slowly and sadly back to my castle.

After that I never felt quite safe at any time. I dared not fire a gun; I dared not build a fire; I dared not walk far from home.

While awake, I was always planning how to escape the savages. While asleep, I was always dreaming of dreadful things.

Yet days and months passed by, and still no other savages came.

I DISCOVER A WRECK

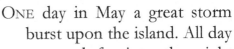

ONE day in May a great storm burst upon the island. All day and far into the night the rain fell and the wind blew, the lightnings flashed, and the thunder rolled.

But I was used to such storms, and I minded it but little. I stayed home in my castle, and felt very thankful that I had a place so safe and dry and comfortable.

I sat up quite late, reading my Bible by the light of a little lamp I had made, and thinking of my strange lot in life. Suddenly I heard a sound which I felt sure was the noise of a gun fired at sea.

I started up quickly. I threw on my raincoat and mounted to my lookout on the top of the great rock.

The rain had stopped and the wind was going down. It was now past midnight, and very dark.

A moment after I had reached my place there was a flash of light that caused me to stop and listen for another gun.

In a few seconds I heard it. It seemed to come from that part of the sea where I was once caught by the strong current and driven far out in my boat.

I knew at once that the shots were fired from some ship in distress. Perhaps she was being driven upon the shore by the wind and waves. Could I do anything to help the poor men on board?

With great labor and danger to myself I gathered some sticks and brush into a pile on the rock and set it on fire.

The wood was not dry, but when the fire was once kindled it blazed up fiercely and cast a light over all the rocks and trees about me.

I felt sure that if there were sailors on the ship, they could not help but see it. And no doubt they did see it, for I soon heard another gun.

All night long I kept the fire burning; but no other sound besides the wind did I hear.

When it was broad day and the mists had cleared away, I turned my spyglass toward that part of the sea from which the sounds came.

Far away from the shore there was surely something; but whether it was a wreck or a ship under sail, I could not tell. The distance was too great.

I watched it from time to time all day. It did not move.

"It must be a ship at anchor," I said to myself.

Early the next morning I took my gun and went down toward that side of the island where the current had once caught me. When I had come to the shore there, I climbed upon some rocks and looked out over the sea.

The air was very clear now, and I could plainly see the ship.

She was not at anchor. She was fast on some great rocks of which there were many in that part of the sea.

I saw that the masts of the vessel were broken, and that her hull was lying more than halfway out of the water.

I thought of the sailors who must have been on board, and wondered if any had escaped. It seemed impossible that any could have reached the shore through the furious sea that was raging during the storm.

"Oh, that one had been saved!" I cried as I walked up and down the shore.

I wrung my hands, my lips were firmly set, my eyes were full of tears.

"Oh, that one had been saved!" I cried again and again.

It was thus that after so many lonely years without seeing a friendly face I longed to have at least one companion to talk with and to share my hopes and fears.

The sea was now quite calm. Even among the rocks the water was smooth.

Seeing everything thus favorable, I made up my mind to get my canoe and go out to the wreck.

I hurried back to my castle to get things ready for my voyage.

I packed a big basket with bread; I filled a jug with fresh water; I put a compass in my pocket that I might have it to steer by; I threw a bag full of raisins upon my shoulder.

Loaded with all these necessary things, I went round to the place where my canoe was hidden. I found her half full of water, for she had been lying there neglected for a long time.

With much labor I bailed the water out of her and got her afloat. Then I loaded my cargo into her, and hurried home for more.

My second load was a bag full of rice, the umbrella to set up over my head for shade, another jug of water, a cheese, a bottle of milk, and about two dozen barley cakes.

All these I carried around to my canoe. If there were men on board the wreck they might be in need of food.

When I had arranged everything in good order, I started out.

I kept the canoe quite close to the shore until I had rounded the point past which the dangerous current flowed. Being then in smooth water, I struck boldly out toward the wreck.

Soon, however, upon looking a little ahead of me, I saw the second current flowing in a great eddy past a long line of half-hidden rocks.

As I looked on these rapid currents, my heart began to fail me. I knew that if I should be driven into one of them, it would carry me a great way out to sea. It would carry me so far that I should never be able to get back again.

Yet I was determined to persevere in my venture.

I MAKE ANOTHER VOYAGE

WITH very great care I steered my canoe out to sea. I kept just within the edge of the current on my right hand. It carried me along at a great rate, but I did not lose control of the canoe.

In about two hours I came up to the wreck. It was a sad sight to look at.

The ship lay partly on her side, and was jammed fast between two great rocks.

She looked like a Spanish ship. She had been badly broken by the waves, and everything on her decks had been swept away.

As I came close to her, a dog looked over her side and barked at me. When I called him he jumped into the sea and swam out to the canoe.

I lifted him on board, and found that he was almost dead with hunger and thirst.

I gave him a barley cake, and he devoured it like a half-starved wolf. I then gave him a little water, but not too much lest he should harm himself. He drank, and then looked up as if asking for more.

After this I went on board. A sad sight met my eyes. For in the cookroom I saw two sailors who had been drowned, with their arms fast around each other.

I suppose that when the ship struck the waves dashed all over her and the men had no way of escape. Those who were not swept overboard were drowned between decks.

Besides the dog there was no other live thing on board.

I found some chests that had belonged to the sailors. With much labor I got two of them into the canoe without stopping to look inside of them.

Besides these chests, I took a fire shovel and tongs, which I needed very much. I found, also, two little brass kettles, a gridiron, and a large copper pot.

The tide was now setting in toward the island again. So, with the few goods I had found and the poor dog, I started for home.

By keeping on the outside of the eddying current I had no trouble in bringing the canoe safe to land. The sun was almost down when I anchored her in a little inlet just off the point of rocks.

I was so tired that I could do nothing more that day. So, after eating my supper, of which I gave the dog a good share, I lay down in the canoe and went to sleep.

I slept very soundly, and did not wake until morning.

In looking over my goods, I made up my mind to store them in my new cave in the woods. For that was much nearer than my home castle.

When I opened the chests I found several things that I was very glad to get.

In one I found two jars of very good sweetmeats. They were so well corked that the salt water had not harmed them. There were two other jars of the same kind; but they were open at the top, and the water had spoiled the sweetmeats.

In the other chest there were some good shirts, which I needed very much. There were also about a dozen and a half of white linen hand-kerchiefs. I was very glad to find these, for they would be pleasant to wipe my face with on a hot day.

In a secret drawer of the first chest I found three bags of Spanish money. I counted eleven hundred pieces of silver.

At the bottom of one of the bags there were six Spanish gold pieces, each worth about fifteen dollars. These were wrapped up in a piece of paper.

At the bottom of the other bag there were some small bars of gold. I suppose there was at least a pound of these yellow pieces.

After all, I got very little by this voyage. I had no use for the money. It was worth no more to me than the dust under my feet. I would have given it all for a pair of good shoes or some stockings for my feet.

After I had carried everything to my cave I took the canoe back to her old harbor on the farther side of the island. Then I returned to my castle, where I found everything in good order.

And now I began to live easily again. I was as watchful as before, and never went from my castle without looking carefully around.

I seldom went to the other side of the island. When I visited my cave in the woods, or went to see my goats, I took good care to be well armed.

I HAVE A QUEER DREAM

Two years passed without any alarms, and I was beginning to think that nothing would ever again happen to disturb the quiet of my life.

One night in the rainy season of March I could not sleep. I lay for hours in my hammock and was not able to close my eyes.

I was thinking, thinking, thinking.

I thought of all that had ever happened to me both before and after my shipwreck.

I thought of my first happy years on the island.

I thought of the fear and care that I had lived in ever since I saw the first footprint in the sand.

Then I thought of my great desire to see my native land once more, and to have friends and companions with whom I could talk.

These thoughts brought to mind the savages of whom I had so great a dread, and I began to ask myself a thousand questions about them.

How far off was the coast from which they came?

Why did they come to my island from so great a distance?

What kind of boats did they have?

With such thoughts as these I lay awake until far in the night. My pulse beat fast, my breath came hard, my nerves were unstrung.

At last, worn out by my very restlessness, I fell asleep.

The same thoughts must have followed me into my dreams, but they took a different form.

I dreamed that I was sitting on the seashore with my gun on my lap and my umbrella by my side.

I was thinking, thinking, thinking. I had never been so sad and lonely.

I was thinking of the home I was never to see again, and of the friends who perhaps had forgotten me.

Suddenly, as I lifted my eyes, I thought I saw two canoes coming toward the island. I ran and hid myself in a grove by the shore.

There were eleven savages in the canoes, and they had with them another savage whom they were going to kill and eat.

But I thought in my sleep that this savage suddenly sprang up and ran for his life.

I thought that he came running to the little grove, to hide himself in it.

Seeing him alone, I arose and met him. I smiled kindly, and tried to make him know that I was his friend.

He threw himself on the ground at my feet. He seemed to be asking my help.

I showed him my ladder and made him go up over the wall.

Then I led him into my castle, and he became my servant.

I thought in my sleep, that I cried aloud for joy and said: "Now I shall escape from this place. For this savage will be my pilot. He will guide me to the mainland. He will tell where to go and what to do. He will help me find my own people."

This thought filled my mind with great joy and while I was still rejoicing I awoke.

What a disappointment it was to find that it was only a dream!

For several days I felt very sad. I was almost ready to give up hope.

Then I remembered my dream; and I said to myself: "If I could only get hold of a savage and teach him to love me, things might turn out just that way. He must be one of their prisoners and I must save him from being eaten; for then it will be easy to win his friendship."

This thought so fixed itself in my mind that I could not get rid of it. Waking or sleeping, I seemed to be always planning to get hold of a savage.

At last I set myself about it in earnest. Almost every day I went out with my gun to see if some of these wild men had not again landed on my island.

I GET HOLD OF A SAVAGE

For a year and a half I kept close watch upon the farther shore of the island as well as upon that nearest to my castle. But not a single savage came near.

One morning in June, however, I had a great surprise.

I was just starting out from my castle when I saw five canoes lying high and dry on the beach not a mile away. There was not a man near them. The people who had come in them were perhaps asleep among the trees.

The number of canoes was greater than I had ever counted upon seeing. For there were always four or six savages in each canoe, and there must now be between twenty and thirty men somewhere on the shore.

I did not know what to think of it. I did not feel brave enough to attack so many.

So I stayed in my castle and made ready to defend myself.

"There is little hope of getting a savage this time," I thought to myself.

I waited a long while, but heard no unusual sound. I grew tired of waiting, and made up my mind to see what was going on.

So, with the help of my ladder, I climbed up to my lookout on the top of the rock. I put my spyglass to my eyes and looked down upon the beach.

Surely enough! there they were. I saw no fewer than thirty naked savages dancing around a fire. I saw that they were broiling meat upon the coals, but I could not tell what kind of meat it was.

As I watched I saw some of the dancers run to a boat and drag two miserable prisoners from it. They must have been in the boat all the time, but as they were lying down I did not see them.

All the dancers now crowded around the poor prisoners. They knocked one of them down with a club, and then fell upon him with their knives. I supposed they were going to cut him up for their horrid feast.

For a few moments they seemed to forget the other prisoner, for they left him standing alone at one side.

All at once he made a break for liberty. You never saw a hound run so fast. He ran along the sandy beach, right toward my castle. I was dreadfully frightened. I thought that now my dream was coming true, and that he would surely hide in my grove.

But would the other part of the dream come true? Would the other savages lose sight of him, and running another way, not come near the castle? I feared not.

However, I stayed in my lookout and watched to see what would happen.

I saw, to my joy, that only three of the savages followed him. He ran so fast that he gained ground on them. If he could hold out for ten or fifteen minutes, he would get away from them all.

Between the savages and my castle there was the little river where I had first landed with my raft.

If the poor fellow could not swim across this stream, he would surely be taken. I watched to see what he would do.

To my surprise the river did not hinder him at all. The tide was up, but he plunged in and with twenty or thirty strokes was across. I had never seen a finer swimmer.

When his pursuers reached the stream, he was already far away. Two of them jumped in and swam across. The other one stood still a minute and then turned softly back. It was lucky for him that he could not swim.

"Now," thought I to myself, "now is the time to get me a savage!"

In another moment I was down in my castle. I picked up my two guns. I was over the wall in less time than it takes me to tell about it. Never once did I think of fear.

I ran swiftly down the hill toward the sea. In another minute I was between the poor captive and his pursuers.

"Hello, there! Come back! I will help you," I cried.

Of course he did not understand a word. But he heard me and looked back. I beckoned to him with my hand, and this he understood better.

There was no time for waiting, however. The two savages that followed were close upon me.

I rushed upon the foremost one and knocked him down with my gun. I did not want to shoot, lest the other savages would hear the noise and come to his rescue.

The second pursuer came, running and panting, only a little way behind. When he saw me, he stopped as if he were frightened. I ran toward him, with my gun to my shoulder.

As I came nearer, I saw that he had a bow and arrow and was taking aim at me. What could I do but shoot? He fell to the ground and never moved again.

I now looked around to see what had become of the poor captive. I saw him standing still and gazing at me. The noise of my gun had frightened him so that he did not know what to do.

I called to him: "Come here, my good fellow! I will not hurt you."

But of course he did not understand. Then I motioned to him with signs. He came a little way and then stopped. He came a little farther and stopped again. He was trembling like a leaf.

No doubt he was afraid that he would be killed as his two pursuers had been.

I spoke kindly to him and made signs that I would not hurt him. He came nearer and nearer, trembling, and kneeling down at almost every step.

I smiled; I looked as pleasant as I could; I made still other signs.

He came quite close to me. He laid his head upon the ground. He took hold of my foot and set it on his neck. This was his way of saying that he would be my slave forever.

I took hold of his hand and lifted him up. I spoke kindly to him.

Thus I at last got hold of a savage, as I had so long desired.

I AM PLEASED WITH MY MAN FRIDAY

THE savage spoke to me. I could not understand his words, but they were very pleasant to hear. For it had now been more than twenty-five years since I had heard the sound of a man's voice.

He pointed to the two savages who had been pursuing him. They were lying on the ground where they had fallen. Both were quite dead.

He could not understand how I had killed the second savage when he was so far away from me. He made signs that I should let him see whether his enemy was really dead or only pretending to be so.

I told him, as well as I could, that he might go to him. He ran to the fallen savage and looked at him. He turned him first on one side and then on the other. He seemed very much puzzled.

Then he picked up the savage's bow and arrows and brought them to me.

I turned to go back to my castle and beckoned him to follow me.

He stood quite still for a moment and then pointed again to the bodies on the ground. By signs he asked me if he might bury them, lest the other savages should come up and find them there. I answered by signs and gave him leave.

The work was quickly done. With a sharp stick and his big hands he soon dug two big holes in the sand. He laid the bodies in them and covered them up. Then he smoothed the sand and patted it down so that no one could see that it had been touched.

Having thus put the two savages out of sight he turned to me again. I motioned him to follow me. But on second thought I did not go back to the castle. I led him far into the woods, to my new cave of which I have told you.

Once inside of that cave, I felt safe.

I gave the poor fellow some bread and a bunch of raisins to eat. I gave him also a drink of water from a jug, and he was so thirsty from running that he came near drinking it all.

Then I showed him a place where I had put some rice straw with a blanket over it. It was quite a good bed, and I myself had sometimes slept upon it.

He seemed to know that I meant for him to lie down there and rest. Soon he was fast asleep.

He was a handsome fellow. He was tall but not too large.

His hair was long and black. His forehead was high and broad. His eyes were very bright.

His face was round and plump. His nose was well shaped. His lips were thin. His teeth were white as ivory.

His skin was not black like that of an African. It was not yellow like that of some Indians. But it was a kind of olive color, very pleasant to look at.

After he had been asleep about an hour he awoke and came out of the cave where I was milking my goats. He made signs to show that he was glad to see me.

Then he laid his head flat down on the ground and set my foot upon it, as he had done before. This was his way of saying that he would do anything I wished.

I understood him and told him by signs that I was well pleased with him.

I spoke some simple words to him and tried to teach him what they meant. He was quick to learn and soon began to try to talk to me.

I named him FRIDAY, because it was on that day of the week that I had saved his life.

He soon learned to call me "Master," and to say "yes" and "no" in the right way.

In the evening I gave him an earthen pot with some milk in it, and showed him how to sop his bread in the milk. I also gave him a barley cake, which he ate as though it was very good.

All that night we stayed in the cave. But early the next morning I led him back to my castle.

My first care was to learn whether the savages had left the island. I climbed to the top of the rock and looked around with my spyglass.

I saw the place where the savages had been. I saw where they had built their fire. But they were not there. I could see no sign of them or of their canoes. It was plain that they had left the place.

I gave my man Friday one of my guns to carry. In his right hand he held my sword, and on his back were his bow and arrows.

I carried two guns myself. And thus armed we went boldly down to the beach.

The sand was red with blood, and bones and bits of flesh were scattered all around. These I caused Friday to gather up and bury.

We stayed on the beach for some time, but could find nothing more.

Friday gave me to understand that there had been three other prisoners in the boats with him. I had no doubt that the savages had killed and eaten them all.

The next day I made a tent for Friday to stay in. It was just inside of my castle wall and in front of the door into my own sleeping room.

As he had no clothes I set to work to make him a suit. I gave him some linen trousers which had belonged to one of our sailors, and which I had not worn because they were too small.

Then I made him a little jacket of goatskin, and from the skin of a rabbit I fashioned a very good cap that fitted his head quite well.

You should have seen him when he was clothed. He was very proud, but oh, so awkward!

He went around with a broad smile on his face. He tried to do everything that was pleasing to me.

And indeed I was much delighted with him. For no man ever had a more faithful servant.

I TEACH FRIDAY MANY THINGS

WHEN my man Friday had been with me three days I took him out hunting.

As we were going through some woods, I saw a wild goat lying under a tree with two young kids sitting by her. I caught hold of Friday.

"Stop," I said. "Stand still."

Then I took aim at one of the kids, shot and killed it.

The noise of the gun so frightened the poor savage that he did not know what to do. He shook like a leaf. He thought that I was going to kill him.

He did not see the kid I had shot. He threw himself at my feet. Although I could not understand a word he said, yet I knew that he was begging me to have pity on him.

And indeed I did pity him—he was so frightened.

I took him by the hand and lifted him up. I laughed at him and pointed to the kid that I had killed. When he saw it and understood me, he ran to fetch it.

Going on through the woods, I saw a big bird sitting on a tree. I thought it was a hawk.

"See there, Friday!" I said, as I pointed to it.

Bang! went my gun. The bird fell to the ground. It was not a hawk, but a parrot.

Friday was amazed. He looked at the gun and trembled.

For a long time he would not touch a gun. He would look at it and talk to it. He would say, in his own language: "O wonderful thing! Do not kill me! Do not kill me!"

We found nothing more in the woods that day. Friday carried the kid home, and I took off its skin and dressed it. Then I stewed some of the best pieces and made some good broth.

At dinner I gave some of the broth to my man. He liked it very well, but he could not bear salt in it.

I tried to show him that food was best with a little salt. But he did not think so, and he would never eat meat that was salted.

The next day I set Friday to work. I had him thrash some barley for me and grind the grains into meal as I had always done.

He did his work very well.

Then I let him see me make some bread and bake it. He learned very fast and soon could cook and keep house as well as any one.

Little, by little I taught him how to work on my farm. We fenced another field and sowed more barley. For now there were two mouths to feed instead of one.

Very soon Friday learned to talk quite well. He learned the name of everything he saw. He was very quick, and I took pleasure in teaching him.

I told him all about gunpowder and guns and showed him how to shoot. I gave him a knife, which pleased him not a little. I made him a belt and gave him a hatchet to carry in it.

I told him about the countries on the other side of the great ocean. And I told him something of my own history.

Little by little I explained how my people traded in great ships, and how my own ship had been wrecked on the coast of this island.

Thus, between working and teaching, I forgot all my fears. The days passed by, and every day brought some new delight.

It was the pleasantest year of my life.

I often asked my man Friday to tell me about his own country. He told me all that he knew, and his words made me feel quite sure that the mainland of South America was not far away.

In fact, the low shore that I could see far to the west of my island was part of the coast of that great continent.

Friday told me that white men sometimes went there. He said that they had long, dark beards and were always trying to trade with his people.

I felt quite sure they were Spaniards, and I had a great mind to go over, if I could, and join them. Indeed, my whole mind was set on seeing some of my own people again.

I thought that if I could only get to the mainland, I would find some way to reach England, or at least some place where Englishmen lived.

At last I told Friday that I would give him a boat to go back to his own country. This was part of my plan for getting away from the island.

I took him over to the other side of the island and showed him my canoe.

We cleared it of water and then took a short sail in it. Friday could paddle very well.

"Now, Friday," I said, "shall we paddle across the sea to your own country?"

He looked very dull at my saying this, and I saw that he thought the canoe was too small.

"Well," I said, "I have a bigger boat. I will show it to you to-morrow."

The next morning, therefore, I took him to see the first boat I had made and which I could not get to the water.

He said it was big enough. But it had been lying on the ground for twenty-three years and was rotten.

"We will make a new boat, Friday," I said. "We will make one as big as this. Then you shall go to your old home in it."

He looked very sad.

"Why are you angry with Friday?" he asked. "What has he done?"

I told him that I was not angry, and asked him what he meant.

"Not angry! not angry!" he cried. "Then why do you want to send Friday away to his old home?"

"Why, Friday," I said, "didn't you say that you wished you were there?"

"Yes, yes," said he. "Friday wishes both were there, but not Friday without his master."

"But what would I do there?" I asked. "I could do nothing."

"Oh, yes, master," he answered very quickly. "You could do much. You could teach wild mans to be tame, to know God, to live right. You could do much."

141

"No, Friday," I said. "You shall go without me. Leave me here to live by myself as I did before."

He looked very sad. Then all at once he ran and picked up a hatchet. He brought it and gave it to me.

"What shall I do with this?" I asked.

"You take it. Kill Friday," he said.

"Indeed," I said, "and why shall I do that?"

"Then why do you send Friday away?" he said. "Better kill than send away."

The tears stood in his eyes as he spoke. I saw that he loved me and would always stand by me.

So I told him that I would never, never send him away, and that he should always stay with me.

You should have seen his eyes brighten.

I MAKE A NEW BOAT

I MADE up my mind to begin the new boat at once.

So, the next day, I went with Friday to find a good tree.

There were trees enough on the island to build a fleet. But, I must find one that was close to the water, so that we could launch the boat when it was made.

At last Friday found one. He knew, better than I, what kind of wood was best for making a boat.

It was an odd-looking tree, and to this day I do not know its name.

Friday chopped it down. He cut off a part of it for the boat.

He wished to build a fire on the top of it and thus burn out the hollow part of the boat.

But I showed him a better way, to chop it out with hatchets and chisels.

In about a month it was finished. With our axes we cut and hewed the outside till it was in a very good shape.

Then we worked hard for two weeks to get the boat into the water.

But when she was in, how well she floated! She would have carried at least twenty men.

It was wonderful how well Friday could manage her. It was wonderful how fast he could paddle.

"Now, Friday," I said, "do you think she will carry us over the sea?"

"Yes, master," he said, "she will carry us even in the worst wind."

My next care was to make a mast and a sail, and to fit the boat with an anchor and a rudder.

It was easy enough to get the mast. I had Friday cut down a tall young cedar that grew near the place.

He shaped it and smoothed it, and made as pretty a mast as you would wish to see.

As for the sail, that was another thing. I had old sails, or pieces of old sails in plenty.

But they had been lying in this place and in that for six and twenty years. It would be a wonder if they were not all rotten.

After a long search I found two pieces which I thought would do. I set to work, patching and stitching.

It was slow work without needles, you may be sure.

At last I had a three-cornered, ugly thing like a shoulder-of-mutton sail to be put up with a boom at its bottom part.

I had also a little short sprit to run up at the top of the mast.

It took two months to make the sails and the rigging as I wished.

Then I put in a rudder to steer the boat. I was a poor carpenter, and I made a pretty rough job of it.

Friday knew how to paddle a canoe as well as any man.

But he knew nothing about a sail. He had never seen a boat steered by a rudder.

We made several little voyages near the island and I taught him how to manage everything about the boat.

Much as I wished to go back to my own people, I could not make up my mind to try the long voyage across to the mainland.

I had now been on the island twenty-seven years. My man Friday had been with me about two years, and these had been the happiest of my life. I had everything to make me comfortable and happy.

Why should I wish to go away?

I had a great longing to see my native land again, to talk with people of my own race, perhaps to visit my kindred once more. This longing I could not rid myself of, day or night.

But now new thoughts came into mind. I felt that in some way I would soon escape from the island. Indeed, I was quite sure that I would not stay there another year.

I cannot tell you what made me feel that way. But I seemed to know that some great change in my life was near at hand.

Yet I went on with my farming as before. I dug, I planted, I reaped, I gathered my grapes, I did everything just as though I had no such thoughts.

My man Friday was the truest of helpers. He did all the heavy labor. He would not let me lift my hand if he could help it.

The rainy season at last came upon us, and this put an end to most of our outdoor work.

We took our new boat to a safe place some distance up the little river, above the point where I had landed my rafts from the ship.

We hauled her up to the shore at high-water mark, and there Friday dug a little dock for her.

This dock was just big enough to hold her and it was just deep enough to give her water to float in.

When the tide was out we made a strong dam across the end of it, to keep the water out. Thus she lay high and dry on the bank of the river.

To keep the rain off we laid a great many branches of trees upon her till she was covered thickly with them. A thatched roof could not have protected her better.

Little did I think that I should never see our boat floating upon the water again. For all that I know, she is still lying high and dry in her little waterproof dock.

We were now kept indoors a great part of the time, but we kept ourselves occupied pleasantly, and the hours passed swiftly.

My first duty every morning was to read several chapters from the Bible. Then I instructed Friday in some of the truths of religion.

I was but an awkward teacher, but I did my best and was honest.

I began by asking him about the Creator.

I asked him who made the sea, the hills, the woods, the ground we walked on.

He told me it was one great being who lived beyond all.

I confess I could not have given a better answer.

He said that this great being was older than the sea or the land, the moon or the stars.

Then I said, "If this being has made all things, why do not all things worship him?"

He looked very grave, and with eyes full of innocence, answered, "All things say O to him."

Thus he taught me while I was trying to teach him.

I SEE A STRANGE SAIL

I PASS over some wonderful things that happened during my last year on the island. For I must not make this story too long.

I was fast asleep in my castle one morning when Friday came running in.

"O master, master!" he cried, "a boat, a boat!"

I jumped up and went out as quickly as I could. I was in such haste that I forgot to carry my gun with me.

I looked toward the sea. About three miles from the shore I saw a strange boat coming to the island. It carried a leg-of-mutton sail and was coming swiftly with the wind. "Surely," I thought, "this is not the kind of boat that savages sail in."

Then I saw that it was coming not from the open sea on my side of the island, but from around a point on the south shore.

I ran back to my castle and told Friday to stay inside and keep quiet till we could learn whether the people in the boat were friends or foes.

Then I climbed up to my lookout on the top of the great rock.

I looked out toward the south shore, and there I saw a ship lying at anchor. As nearly as I could guess, it was about five miles from my castle and at least three miles from the shore.

It looked just like an English ship, and the boat was surely an English longboat.

I cannot tell you how glad I was at the thought that some of my own countrymen were so near. Yet I felt strange fears, and so made up my mind to be very cautious.

In the first place, what business could an English ship have in these seas? The English had no lands in this part of the world. They would not come here to trade. There had been no storms to drive the vessel to this place.

The more I thought of the matter, the more I doubted. If these people were indeed English, they must be here for no good purpose.

By this time the boat was quite near the shore. I could see the men in it quite plainly. They looked like Englishmen.

As they came in the tide was at its highest, and so they ran the boat far up on the beach about half a mile from me.

I now counted eleven men, and all but three were armed with swords. As soon as the boat touched the land, the most of them jumped out.

Then I saw that the three unarmed men were prisoners. Their hands were tied behind them and they were closely guarded.

As they were led on shore, they seemed in great distress as though begging for their lives.

When Friday saw all this, he cried out to me, "O master! the white mans do just like savage mans with their prisoners."

"Why, Friday," I said, "do you think they are going to eat them?"

"Yes, yes," he answered, "they are going to eat them."

The prisoners were led far up on the beach, and I expected every moment to see them killed.

But soon their guards seemed to change their minds. They talked together for a little while. Then they untied the prisoners' hands and let them go where they pleased.

The seamen scattered, some going this way, some that, as though they wished to see the country. But the men who had been prisoners sat down on the ground and seemed very sad and full of despair.

I thought then of the time when I had first landed on that shore—how I had no hope, and how I gave myself up for lost.

As I have said, the tide was at its highest when the men came on shore. They rambled around till it had flowed out and left their boat high and dry on the sand.

They had left two men with the boat to guard it. But the weather being very warm, these men had fallen asleep.

When one of them awoke and found the water far out from the boat, he began to hello for help. All the men came running and tried to drag the boat out to the water.

But it was so heavy they could not move it. They tugged and pulled for a long time. Then I heard one of them shout: "Let her alone, boys! She'll float all right when the next tide comes up."

With that they gave it up and all strolled out into the country again.

I MAKE A BOLD RESCUE

I KNEW that the tide would not be at its highest again before night. So I thought that I would arm myself, and, as soon as it was dark, would venture out and learn more about my strange visitors if I could.

I looked at my guns and got everything ready, and then sat down to wait.

The day, as I have said, was very hot. The three men who had been prisoners still sat under a tree by the shore. But all the rest were in the woods. No doubt they would rest in some shady place until the sun went down.

At about two o'clock I became so uneasy that I could wait no longer.

"Friday," I said, "let us go out and see what we can do."

You should have seen us as we marched out of the castle.

I had two guns on my shoulders and Friday had three. I had on my goatskin coat and my great hat that I have told you about. At my side was a naked sword, and in my belt were two huge pistols.

I must have looked very fierce.

We went quietly down the hill, keeping ourselves hidden among the trees. At last, when we were quite near the three men, I jumped suddenly out before them and cried, "What are you, gentlemen?"

Never were men more surprised.

They sprang to their feet, but they could not speak a word. In fact, they were on the point of running away from me when I cried: "Hold, gentlemen! Do not be afraid. I am a friend. I bring help."

"Then, indeed," said one of them, "you must have been sent from heaven; for our case is hopeless."

"All help is from heaven, sir," I said; and then I briefly told them how I had seen them brought to the shore.

"I am an Englishman," I said, "and I stand ready to help you. I have one servant, and we are well armed. Tell us what is your case, and how we may serve you."

"Our case," said the foremost of the three men, "is too long to tell you now; for our enemies are very near. I was the captain of the ship that lies at anchor offshore. Three days ago the sailors all rose against me. They made me their prisoner. They seized upon the ship, for they wanted to become pirates.

"They were about to kill me; but this morning they decided to leave me on this island to die. The men who are with me, they are doomed to the same fate. One is my mate, the other a passenger.

"Being brought ashore here, we had no hope but to perish. For it did not seem to us that any one could live in such a desolate place."

"But where are those cruel enemies of yours?" I asked. "Do you know where they are gone?"

"They are there, sir," he said, pointing to a grove not far away. "They are sleeping in the shade. If they should wake and see you with us, they would kill us all."

"Have they any firearms?" I asked.

"Only two muskets," he answered, "and one of these they have left in the boat."

"Then trust everything to me," I said. "If they are asleep it will be easy to kill them all. But I think it will be better to make them our prisoners."

The captain then told me that there were two very wicked fellows among them who were the ringleaders.

"It is they who have made all this trouble," he said. "If they and two others could be overcome the rest would come back and do their duty. Indeed, I am sure that many of them have gone into this business against their will."

I HAVE AN ANXIOUS DAY

WHILE we were talking we had slowly withdrawn among the trees where we were sheltered from sight.

The captain promised me that if we should succeed in getting control of the ship, he would do anything that I wished. He would carry me to England or to any other part of the world. He would live and die with me.

"Well, then," said I, "if you will all obey my commands, we will see what can be done."

I gave each one of them a musket, with powder and shot. I told them to kill as few of the ruffians as they could, and to make prisoners of them all if possible.

Just then we heard some of them awake. In a moment thee men came out of the grove and started down to the shore.

"Are these the ringleaders?" I asked.

"No," answered the captain.

"Well, then, let them go," I said; "but if the rest escape, it will be your fault."

With a musket in his hand and a pistol in his belt, the captain started forward. I was close at his side, while Friday and the other two men went a little ahead of us.

The mate in his eagerness chanced to step on some dry sticks which broke with a sharp noise beneath his feet. One of the seamen, hearing this, looked out and saw us.

He gave the alarm. The sleeping wretches awoke and sprang to their feet. But it was too late. Our guns were already upon them.

I need not tell you of the fight. It was sharp and short.

At its close the two ruffians who had caused all this trouble were lying dead upon the ground. The three other men, who were but slightly hurt, were our prisoners. As for my little army of five, not one was so much as scratched.

While the captain and I were binding the prisoners, Friday and the mate ran to the boat and brought away the oars and the sails.

Soon the three men who had gone down the shore came hurrying back to see what was the matter.

When they saw how matters stood, they at once gave themselves up and were bound with the rest. So our victory was complete.

We now retired to the castle.

The prisoners were led into the back part of the cave that I had first dug, and were left there with Friday as their guard.

With the captain, the mate, and the passenger, I went into my best room, where we all refreshed ourselves with such food as I had at hand.

We had now time to talk over the past and make plans for the future.

I told the captain my whole history just as I have told it to you. He, in his turn, related to me the story of his voyage from England to the West Indies, and how his crew, wishing to become pirates, had seized upon the ship and made him their prisoner.

"There are still twenty-six men on board," he said. "They are no doubt wondering what has become of their fellows. After a while some of them will be likely to come on shore to find out what is the matter."

"Let them come," I said. "We will be ready for them."

We therefore went down to the shore where the boat was still lying.

We found in it some rum, a few biscuits, a horn of powder, and five or six pounds of sugar. This last was very welcome to me, for I had not tasted sugar for several years.

All these things we carried on shore. Then we knocked a big hole in the bottom of the boat.

To tell the truth, I had but little hope that we would ever recover the ship. But I thought that after she had sailed away we might repair the boat. Then we could no doubt make our way to the Spanish settlements on the mainland.

About an hour before sunset, we heard a gun fired from the ship.

"It is as I told you," said the captain.

We saw a signal waving from the mast. Then several other shots were fired.

At last, when there was no answer either to the signals or to the guns there was a great stir on board, and the other boat was launched.

I watched them with my spyglass.

As the boat neared the shore, we saw that there were ten men in her and that they were all armed with muskets.

The sun shone in their faces and we had a good sight of them as they came.

The captain knew them all. He said that there were three very honest fellows among them who had gone into this business against their will. All the rest, however, were bad men who were ready to do any wicked deed.

We now set free two of our prisoners, for they seemed to be trustworthy men and glad that matters had turned in the captain's favor.

"Can we trust them, Captain?" I asked.

"I will stand good for them," said the captain.

I gave them each a gun. We had now seven armed men to meet the ten who were coming to the shore.

But we kept ourselves hidden and waited to see what they would do.

As soon as they reached the shore they ran to see the other boat. What was their surprise to find her stripped of everything and a hole in her bottom.

They shouted, but no one answered.

They fired off their muskets, making the woods ring with their echoes. But still there was no answer.

Then they launched their boat again, and all started to the ship.

But on the way they changed their minds. It would never do, they thought, to leave their friends on the island without so much as hunting for them.

They therefore rowed back to the shore. Three men were left with the boat as guards, and the rest started out into the country to seek their lost companions.

We should have been glad if they had come our way, so that we might have fired on them; but this they failed to do.

Night was fast coming on, and they did not dare to go far from the shore.

By and by they came back to the boat again.

We feared that they had given up the search and would now return to the ship.

The sun was setting, and darkness would soon cover both land and sea.

I AM CALLED GOVERNOR

By my orders, Friday and the captain's mate hurried through the woods to the little river where I had landed so long ago with my rafts.

When they had reached the place, they shouted as loudly as they could.

The men who were just getting into the boat heard them. They answered, and ran along the shore toward the little river.

The three who had been left in the boat also rowed around toward the same place. Near the mouth of the river, however, they came to land again, and one of them ran along the bank of the stream to meet his fellows.

At this moment I rushed forward with the captain, and seized the boat before the two fellows who were in it could save themselves.

It was now almost dark, and we had nothing to do but wait till the seamen came back to the shore to look for their boat.

Soon Friday and the captain's mate rejoined us, and I stood at the head of my little army, listening to the seamen as they made their way through the bushes.

We could hear them calling to one another. We could hear them telling how lame and tired they were. We could hear them saying that they were in an enchanted island where there were witches and other kinds of uncanny things. All this pleased us very much.

By and by they came to the shore, quite close to where we were standing.

One of the men whom they had left in the boat was standing with us. He was one of the honest men whom the captain had pointed out, and he had joined us very gladly.

By my orders he now cried out, "Tom Smith! Tom Smith!" For that was the name of the leader of the company.

Tom Smith answered at once, "Is that you, Robinson?" for he knew the voice.

"Yes," the other answered, "and for God's sake, Tom Smith, throw down your arms and yield, or you will all be dead men the next minute."

"To whom must we yield?" cried Tom Smith. "Where are they?"

"Here they are," was the answer. "Here's our captain at the head of a whole army of fighting men. The boatswain is dead, and Bill Fry is dead, and all the rest of us are prisoners. If you don't yield, you are lost."

"If they'll give us quarters, we'll yield," said Smith.

Then the captain himself spoke up. "You, Smith," he said, "you know my voice. If you lay down your arms at once, you shall have your lives—all but Will Atkins."

Upon this, Will Atkins cried out: "For God's sake, Captain, give me quarter! What have I done? I have been no worse than the rest."

Now this was not true. For it was Will Atkins who had first laid hold of the captain, and it was he who had tied the captain's hands.

"Nay, Will Atkins," said the captain. "You know what you have done, and I can promise you nothing. You must lay down your arms and trust to the governor's mercy."

By "the governor" he meant me, Robinson Crusoe—for they called me governor.

The upshot of the whole matter was that they all laid down their arms and begged for their lives.

Then I sent three of my men to bind them with strong cords, which they did, much to my joy.

After that I sent my great army of *fifty* men— which, after all, were only five besides the three who already had them in charge—to lead them to prison.

I told the captain that it would be better to put some of our prisoners in one place and some in another, as then they would be less likely to try to escape.

He and Friday therefore took Atkins with two others who were the worst to my cave in the woods. It was a dismal place, but very safe. There the rough fellows were left with their hands and feet tied fast, and the door blocked up with a huge stone.

Late as it was, I sent the rest of them to my bower. As they also were bound, and as the place was fenced in and was very strong, they were quite safe there.

They were all much frightened. For they believed that the island was inhabited by English- men, and that the governor had really a large army. They felt that the better they behaved the safer they would be.

The captain went out to talk with them.

"My men," he said, "you all know what a great crime you have committed. You are now in the power of the governor of this island. He will send you to England. There you will be tried, and you will be hanged in chains."

At these words they turned pale and groaned. For they were but young men and had been led into this by the four or five ruffians who were the ringleaders.

"Now, my men," the captain went on, "you know that I have always been kind to you."

"Certainly you have," said Tom Smith.

"Aye, aye!" cried all the rest.

"Well, then," said the captain, "it grieves my heart to see you in this hard case. The ship, as you know, still lies at anchor off the shore. It is still held by some of the ruffians who brought this trouble upon us. If I should persuade the governor to set you free, what say you? Would you help me retake the ship?"

"Aye, aye!" they all cried. "We would stand by you to the end, for we should then owe our lives to you."

"Well, then," said the captain, "I will see what I can do. I will go and talk with the governor."

The matter was soon arranged.

The captain was to choose five of those he thought would be most faithful. These were to help him retake the ship. But the rest were to stay in prison as hostages.

If the five behaved themselves well, then all were to be set free. If they did not behave, then all were to be put to death.

These were the governor's orders.

It was then agreed that the captain, with all the men he could trust, should go out to the ship. I and my man Friday were to stay on shore to watch the prisoners.

The hole in the bottom of the long boat was soon mended. Four men, with the passenger as their leader, went out in this. The captain, with five men, went out in the other boat.

It was after midnight when they reached the ship.

The men on board were taken by surprise, for they thought that these were their friends who were but just then returning to the ship.

They even threw a rope to them and helped them on board, never suspecting that anything was wrong.

The whole business was managed well. The second mate and the carpenter, who were among the leaders in the plot, were soon overpowered.

The rebel captain, the worst of the crew, was asleep in his berth. He sprang up and showed fight. He shot three times at the captain's party, wounding the mate but touching no one else.

The mate, wounded as he was, raised his musket and fired. The rebel captain fell to the deck with a bullet through his head.

The rest, seeing that they were without leaders, fell upon their knees and begged for their lives.

Thus the captain became again the master of his own ship.

I HAVE A NEW SUIT OF CLOTHES

 THE next morning I slept quite late in my hammock, for the night had been full of toil and I had had but little rest.

All at once I was awakened by the sound of a gun.

Then I heard some one calling me, "Governor! Governor!" It was the captain's voice.

I hurried out.

He grasped my hand and pointed to the sea. There, a little way from our beach, was the ship.

The weather being fair, the men had brought her around and anchored her near the mouth of the river.

"My dear friend," cried the captain, "there is your ship! She is all yours, for we owe our lives to you. We also are yours. Everything on board of her is yours."

I was ready to sink down with surprise.

For here was a large ship, at last, ready to carry me wherever I wished to go.

At first I could not answer him.

We stood for some minutes with our arms around each other, and neither of us could speak.

At last I broke out, crying like a child. Then we rejoiced together.

When he had talked awhile, the captain told me that he had brought me a present.

"Bring up the box for the governor!" he cried to his men.

They came up the hill, carrying a wooden chest. When it was put down in my castle the captain bade me open it and help myself to all that was inside it.

I did so.

I found first two pounds of good tobacco, then twelve pieces of beef, six pieces of pork, a bag of peas, a box of sugar, a box of flour, a bag full of lemons, and two bottles of lime juice.

But under these was the greatest surprise. There I found six new shirts, six neckties, two pairs of gloves, a pair of shoes, a pair of stockings, a hat, and a very good suit of clothes.

I could now dress like a man again.

I went about it at once. It had been so long since I had worn such clothes that I was very awkward at putting them on.

But at last I came out fully dressed. Friday did not know me. I hardly knew myself.

The next day all was in readiness to sail away.

The second mate, the carpenter, and other ruffians who had been foremost in the rebellion were to be left on the island. In fact, I had put the matter to them in such a way that they requested this as a favor.

"It will be better to stay here than be taken to England to be hanged," I said to them.

I left with them a keg of powder, three muskets, and three swords.

I told them also about my goats, and how I managed them—how I milked them and made butter and cheese.

I showed them my fields of barley and rice.

I showed them, also, my castle, my cave in the woods, and my bower.

"All these are yours," I said.

"They are much more than we deserve," said the second mate; and I agreed with him.

I BRING MY TALE TO A CLOSE

AND SO on the 19th of December, 1687, we set sail for England. I had been on the island twenty-eight years, two months, and nineteen days.

I took on board with me the money that had been by me so long and had been so useless.

I took also my big goatskin cap and my umbrella. Neither did I forget my good Poll Parrot.

As for my man Friday, nothing in the world could have parted him from me. He would have gone to the ends of the earth with me.

The voyage was a long and hard one. But on the eleventh day of June we at last reached London. Once more I was in England, the land of my birth.

I was as perfect a stranger as if I had never been there.

I went down to York. My father and mother had been dead a long time. The friends of my boyhood had forgotten me.

I was alone in the world. Where should I go and what should I do?

By chance I learned that my plantation in Brazil was doing well. The man whom I had left in charge of it had made much money from the tobacco he had raised.

He was an honest man, and when he heard that I was still alive he wrote me a long, kind letter. In this he gave me a full account of the business.

He also sent me a large amount of money, which I was very glad to get.

I was now a rich man. I might have settled down to a life of ease and idleness; but such was not my wish.

Soon I was wandering from one place to another, seeing more of the world. I had many surprising adventures, I assure you; but I need not tell you about them. You would think any account of them very dry reading compared with the story I have already related.

And so, looking back with regretful memories to the years which I spent on my dear desert island, I bid you a kind good-by.

The story of Robinson Crusoe is ended. There is nothing further in this book for the children to read. That which follows is for grown-up people.

TO DANIEL DEFOE, ESQ.

HONORED SIR:

If he who adds to the enjoyment of others is deserving of happiness and high rewards, surely you have won no mean place among those who are blessed. For who has done more for the harmless entertainment of mankind than you with your immortal "Robinson Crusoe?" It is now nearly two hundred years since your fertile fancy invented that story of marvelous though not impossible adventures. You wrote it not for boys, but for men of mature minds. You would doubtless have scorned the thought of composing a book for children. And yet how many millions of boys have remembered and blessed you for having written that one tale!

Your book has had a great history. I imagine that you wrote it hurriedly, at spare moments, while more important duties were pressing upon you; for it bears all the marks of hasty, not to say careless, composition. It is said that you had some trouble in finding a publisher for it, and I do not wonder. A manuscript so faulty in punctuation, in grammar, in all the externals that go to make up a work of art, would have to go begging a long time nowadays! But it was the internal quality of your work that counted. When it was published, people liked it. They talked about your "Robinson Crusoe," they read it and reread it, the boys took to it, and every year it grew in popularity. Your plain, easy, everyday English made it a favorite among the common people who had no use for the higher forms of literary art. Then you had such a knack of making everything appear so real! Your readers never thought of poor Robinson as a creature merely of your imagination; they thought of him as a living personage, they felt acquainted with him as with no other hero of fiction. Your book, therefore, lived. It was reprinted and reprinted again. Thousands of editions were sold. It was translated into every language in which books are printed. In our time no library is complete without it, and no boy is considered a healthy boy who has not tried to read it.

I say *tried* to read it; for who, in this busy age, has succeeded in reading the half of those six hundred pages or more that compose your original work? Who, indeed, among your millions of admirers, has perused even a small portion of the story without skipping numerous paragraphs, perhaps whole pages? You had the knack of spinning things out to their greatest length. You liked to dwell upon incidents that were trivial and unimportant. You felt impelled to preach an occasional sermon by giving up whole pages to your hero's tedious reflections on moral and religious subjects. In your day, when books were few and time was long, all this was very proper; it was no doubt just what your readers expected and relished. But you lived in the eighteenth century, and things have changed since then. Now there are thousands of books to be read, to say nothing of the newspapers; and there is so much to be done that we must make use of the moments in many various ways. We must read as we run. We prefer to waste our time upon the frivolous rather than upon the tedious. We must be interested. The meditations of an imaginary hero seem to us neither instructive nor entertaining. The upshot of the whole matter is that people do not read "Robinson Crusoe" now as they did a few years ago. He who is not a judicious skipper will most likely be bored by your long-windedness and drop the book before he has finished the half of it.

Again, who cares a fig for what Robinson did before he was shipwrecked, or for what he did after his return to England? The life on the desert island, that is the pith and the kernel of the whole story. If you had been writing for twentieth-century readers, you would have said very little about those other matters; you would have gone down to the kernel promptly, and when you had finished with it you would have stopped.

Now in our schools we are doing that which would have astonished the schoolmasters of your day. We are teaching our children to read by putting into their hands books which they cannot help but want to read. Our babes are getting at the very cream of the world's literature. They are draining it off so fast that the more cautious among us begin to wonder if there will be only the skimmed milk for them when they have grown to man's estate. You would be astonished to hear our eight-year-olds discuss old Æsop, old Homer, and many a modern poet and prose writer of whom you know nothing.

They discuss you, also, and they try to read your "Robinson Crusoe." But it is hard reading, and there is so much skipping to be done that when they have finished a portion of it they have not so fine an opinion of the story as you might suppose. It is plain, as I have already hinted, that you did not write for readers of so tender years.

Now I have read in the preface to an early edition of your book all that you say about the abridging of your work. You declare that such an act is "as scandalous as it is knavish and ridiculous." This, however, was addressed to your eighteenth-century readers and not to us of this much later day. If you were living now, you would certainly think more kindly of it; for which is better, to be abridged or to be skipped? So sure am I of your approval that I have not only abridged your story, but I have written it anew for children. Should it be said that I have taken too great liberties with an immortal classic, my plea shall be that I have merely acted the part of a translator. The story remains yours. The ideas are yours; the main points of the narrative are exactly as you put them; the honor of the invention is wholly yours.

181

While preserving your simplicity of style, I have used only such words and expressions as are easiest understood by children in their second or third year at school. Sometimes they are yours, but oftener they are my own. I have softened the harsher parts of your story, so as not to blunt the gentler instincts of our young readers by dwelling too long among scenes of blood and deeds of villainy. I have, passed over those tiresome reflections and moralizings, which you so confidently tell us are "the greatest Beautys" of your work; for, like certain other beauties of your time, their day is past and they have no longer any charm or influence. In short, I have given your story a twentieth-century form for a twentieth-century purpose. I have written it anew in order that children may get to the kernel of it at once without the bother of tearing away the husks. Is it too much to hope that they will thus be led, not only to an easier understanding of "Robinson Crusoe," but also to a deeper appreciation of its worthy and world-famous author, Daniel Defoe?

With these explanations, I trust that you will accept my apologies and will regard my well-meant efforts as neither "scandalous," "knavish," nor "ridiculous." For, whatever may be the fate of my work, the fame of yours has long been assured, and it is plainly impossible for me to diminish in the slightest degree the honor that is justly your due as the creator of "Robinson Crusoe."

J. B.